LUCKY IN LOVE
A FUR-EVER VETERINARY ROMANCE

CARA MALONE

Copyright © 2020 by Cara Malone

All rights reserved.

No part of this book may be reproduced in any form or by any electronic or mechanical means, including information storage and retrieval systems, without written permission from the author, except for the use of brief quotations in a book review.

ACKNOWLEDGMENTS

Many thanks to my editor, Claire Jarrett, who always helps me tell the best story possible.

Thanks to everyone who provided input, voted on cover designs, and procrastinated with me over adorable bunny pictures on social media.

And as always, thank you to my readers and friends in the lesfic community. You're the best!

1
JULES

"Everybody at their cutest today?" Jules Wakefield asked as she walked down the long aisle of rabbit stalls in the barn, dropping handfuls of lettuce into bowls along the way. "Cotton, you're looking a little shaggy with that spring coat coming in. How about working on that this morning? Bugs, we're not going to have any more embarrassingly public amorous incidents, are we?"

Jules spoke sternly to the little chocolate-brown lop, who stood on his hind paws and looked up at her with curiosity.

"Oh, who could stay mad at you, ya little horn dog?" she relented, reaching down and scratching Bugs behind the ears.

There were just under two dozen rabbits in the barn, each one waiting patiently for his or her forever home. The barn could hold as many as fifty, and Jules had plenty of memories from her childhood when it had been at capacity – although even her bunny-crazy mom would admit that fifty rabbits was a handful, to say the least.

These days, Jules was on her own and taking in as few rescues as she could because there were only so many hours in the day and she was only one person. The last thing she wanted while she was trying to sell her parents' property and juggle her own veterinary practice was a barn full to the rafters with these adorable little handfuls.

She'd rescued ten rabbits in the last six months, and found permanent homes for about the same number. It was hard work, time-consuming, but worth it. For as long as Jules could remember, there had been bunnies in her life.

Her parents started rescuing them in their twenties, taking rabbits in from all over the county and adopting them as their own. When they realized that there were no shelters in the area that accepted rabbits and that they couldn't personally adopt all the rabbits that needed homes, Wakefield Rabbit Rescue was born. Jules was ten when the sign went up over the barn, making it official.

Back then, the rescue was her life as much as it was her parents'. She used to lovingly decorate individual name tags for each rabbit as soon as they came to the rescue, observing their personalities and making the artwork match. These little works of art hung on the front of each stall in the barn, and they went with the rabbits to their new homes when they were adopted.

These days, Jules barely had enough time to get out here twice a day to feed and clean the rabbits, but she still did her best to keep up with the name tags. Bugs had a crudely drawn Bugs Bunny on his. Jules had hot-glued a ball of cotton to Cotton's name tag — both were a little on the nose, maybe, but it was better than a quickly scribbled name with no individual touch at all.

It had been six months since she saw her mother on the floor of the barn, trying to teach a bunny how to play with toys. Six months since she'd last seen her dad, a great big statue of a man, cuddling a little furry bunny to his chest and gingerly kissing the top of its head.

They were gone, but the rabbits were still here and Jules wasn't sure how much longer she could keep juggling all of it. It wasn't just the drives out from town, or the time away from her own job. It was the stab in the chest she felt every time she looked at the rabbits and remembered how much they'd meant to her parents, who were gone forever, unfairly ripped from her life.

That was why she needed to sell the house and the rescue along with it, so she could stop coming back here twice a day to rip her own heart out.

"Okay, everybody," she said when she'd gotten to the end of the aisle and her lettuce basket was empty. "On your best behavior today, got it? There's a nice couple coming to see the property and we gotta impress them."

Maybe if they got bowled over by the cute factor of so many bunnies up on their back feet, begging for treats, they wouldn't stop to think about just how much work it took to keep them all fed, happy and healthy.

It wasn't that she wanted to deceive anyone. She'd told every single prospective buyer in the last five months the truth – that her parents had kept the rescue open on a wing and a prayer. And every single one of them so far had turned on their heels and run... a sensible decision, in Jules' estimation.

The rescue was just barely self-sustaining thanks to adoption fees and donations, and the fact that Jules did all the necessary veterinary work pro bono, but there was never going to be any profit in animal rescue. People like her parents did the work for love, not money, but they still had to pay their bills, and their mortgages, and the margins around here were as tight as they came.

In fact, the *only* viable offer Jules had gotten since she put the property up for sale last November was from a real estate developer who saw how the little town of Camden had been booming all around her parents' property, which sat on nearly forty acres of land. The developer, some hot shot from a firm called Manning and Manning Realty, wanted to tear down the house Jules had grown up in, along with the barn and everything else, evict the rabbits and build a housing development.

She'd turned him down cold. The only thing that would hurt more than coming out here every single day and being reminded of her loss was watching her parents' legacy be literally torn down to the ground.

That was why she had to find a buyer who was willing to continue operating the rescue – and fast, before she dropped from exhaustion, grief or both. Jules was only thirty years old but she couldn't keep up this pace forever.

She let out a sigh as she hung the basket on its usual hook by the door, then headed out of the barn to make sure everything was in order around the rest of the property. She pulled weeds and swept the steps leading up to the two-story farmhouse where she'd grown up. She made the place look as tidy and homey as possible, without actually setting foot inside the house – she hadn't done that since her parents' wake.

Her real estate agent had told her it was a mistake to leave all her parents' "knickknacks and clutter" in the house while it was being shown.

"People want houses that feel like *their* new home," she'd explained to Jules. "They don't want to see other people's pictures hanging on the walls, or feel like they just stepped into somebody else's life."

Jules had tried to go inside a couple of times to hide those personal touches away, but every time she did, she hadn't lasted more than five minutes in there. It felt like the house was frozen in time, like her dad might come up from his basement workshop any minute, sawdust on his hands. She could almost smell her mother's Sunday pot roast wafting through the air from the kitchen. And to change anything about the house felt like she was evicting her parents' memory.

She'd just have to wait for a buyer who could look past all those relics of her old life. Maybe today would be the day.

The one part of the house that she could endure was the small screened-in porch on the back of the house. It was where her parents liked to give the bunnies exercise on days when it was too hot to be in the sun, and where the three of them had spent many a spring and summer night looking out on the vast fields behind the property.

Jules was on the porch, dusting the furniture, when she heard a high-pitched, familiar voice call from the front of the house, "Knock-knock! Anybody home?"

"Coming!" she called. She tossed the duster into a drawer and ran her fingers through her dark hair, about cheekbone-length and falling around her eyes, then looked down at her jeans. Dusty and fur-covered from being in the barn with the rabbits, but such was life at a rescue. She brushed herself off as best she could and sent out a quick prayer to the prospective buyers. *Please buy my parents' house.*

Then she went down the steps to the dirt yard and walked around to the front of the house, where a Realtor and a young couple stood.

"Hi, Emmy," Jules greeted the middle-aged agent in the gold jacket. "Good to see you again."

She knew Emmy well by now. She'd brought quite a few prospective buyers to the property, and besides that, she had a big, wrinkly mastiff named Charles that she brought to Jules' clinic once a month to have his claws trimmed.

It was like that with a lot of people who lived in town – if Jules didn't know them simply as a result of living in Camden all her life, then the chances were good that she'd meet them through their pet sooner or later.

"Pleasure's mine," Emmy said, shaking Jules' hand. She introduced her to the couple. "Jules Wakefield, this is Jon Harris and his wife, Amelia."

"Nice to meet you," Jules said. "Emmy told you about the rabbit rescue?"

"Yes," Amelia said, her eyes lighting up. "Truthfully, we weren't really looking for a place that's this... rural... but when we learned about the rescue, I insisted on checking it out."

"Well, Camden is booming these days," Emmy said. "We're getting an Amazon Fulfillment Center, you know. Lots of jobs will come out of that."

Jules had to suppress the urge to snort. Every real estate agent she'd come in contact with in the last few months was talking up the fulfillment center like it would be the thing that finally put Camden on the map. They all said that about the Walmart when it came a few years ago, but who knew? Maybe they were right – Camden was more crowded than ever, and Jules' vet clinic was booming like never before.

"Well, let's not waste any of your time," Jules said. "I'll show you the rabbit barn first."

That was a little white lie. Really, she didn't want to waste her *own* time. The more of it that she spent out here with bunnies and prospective buyers, the less she had to see her own furry patients. She used to do quite a bit of large animal treatment, servicing the many farms in the area, but lately she was seeing more and more dogs, cats and other pets too.

Jules had learned pretty early on in the process of selling the property that a turn-of-the-century farmhouse made a lot of people drool, but not many of them were truly prepared for the realities of rabbit husbandry.

Rabbit urine could be quite potent, for example, and their stalls had to be freshened up every day.

And while some of the rescues, like Jack the lionhead, were adorable little cuddle-bugs, others were skittish and defensive after coming from abusive or neglectful situations. Rabbits needed a lot more care and attention than most people realized, and certainly more time than Jules had to give them these days... but she wouldn't let just anyone take over the rescue. It had to be the right buyer.

The Harrises were hard to read. Jon wrinkled his nose at the smell when they passed a compost pile on the way to the barn, and Jules explained, "Rabbit manure makes great fertilizer, and there's a free, never-ending supply of it around here."

"What do you use it for?" he asked, actually looking a little green around the gills – not a great sign.

"The garden, mostly," Jules said, and he turned even greener.

"A *vegetable* garden?" he asked.

Jules wanted to laugh and ask him what kind of fertilizer he thought grocery store produce grew from, but she figured he wouldn't want to buy the house if she made him vomit during the showing.

"Well, it's the rabbits' food," Jules explained. "My parents started growing all the greens the rabbits eat about fifteen years ago, and there's a field of Timothy grass growing behind the barn to harvest for hay. The rescue needs to operate as leanly as possible and right now, it's about eighty percent self-sustainable."

"That's really cool!" Amelia said. She seemed more

enthusiastic about everything than her husband, her eyes lighting up every time she learned something new. If it were just her, Jules thought she could probably handle it... but with a reluctant partner, the odds of long-term success weren't good.

Jules showed them the barn and let them hold a few rabbits she knew wouldn't bite or scratch – Bugs and Thumper. Amelia walked down the row, smiling at all the bunnies and admiring their name tags, while Jules gave them an idea of what it took to keep the place running and how many rabbits came through every year.

Then she let Emmy give them a tour of the house, going back to the porch and waiting while the three of them talked it all over. It was only April but it was already gearing up to be a hot summer. Jules grabbed a bottle of water from the mini-fridge her parents always kept stocked on the porch. She sat in her dad's favorite glider, a heavy old Amish-built bench that looked out on the Timothy field, and behind that, rows of freshly planted corn in the fields that Jules' parents always leased to the neighboring farmer and which Jules continued to do.

What she was looking at was her parents' legacy – something that, in an ideal world, she would be carrying on herself. That wasn't going to happen – maybe if her parents hadn't passed so suddenly and she'd had time to get used to the idea of life without them. But the best she could do now was put a condition on the sale: the rescue must continue to operate, and it must retain its name – her family's name.

She hadn't bothered to mention that detail to Amelia and Jon because she could tell before the showing was even halfway over that they weren't going to make an offer. She'd developed a bit of a sixth sense about these things after five months of unsuccessful showings.

Sure enough, about ten minutes went by and Jules heard a car crunch its way out of the gravel driveway, and then Emmy appeared and joined her on the glider.

"They left?" Jules asked. Emmy nodded and Jules reached for the mini-fridge. "Water?"

"Thanks," Emmy said.

"Let's hear it."

"They think it's a really nice property," Emmy told her. She always tried to soften the blow, unlike some of the other real estate agents in town, who didn't even bother to stick around and talk to Jules after showings.

"But?"

"It's more work than they're interested in. They're city folk," Emmy said. She took a long sip of water and Jules knew she had more to say. She waited patiently and finally, Emmy added, "...and they're not sure the investment will pay out."

Yeah. Jules had heard that before, from other real estate agents and from Marissa, the estate attorney her parents had hired to handle their will. She knew it was the truth, too – the house was historic, the land was extensive, but the rabbit rescue was like an anchor dragging the value of the whole property down.

"Nobody can afford to take a mortgage out on a property that has a business that doesn't make money," Jules said.

"Bingo," Emmy said. "Sorry, hon."

Jules shook her head. "It's fine – nothing I haven't heard before. I was just hoping for a miracle is all."

She'd spent the last six months hoping that someone would come along and see the rescue with the same optimistic eyes that her parents had. The problem was that the rescue was a full-time operation and any buyer would have to be independently wealthy to run it *and* make the hefty mortgage payments. Jules' parents had worked hard to pay their own loans off in their forties so they could quit their day jobs and dedicate themselves entirely to the rescue, but Jules couldn't just *give* the property away…

She sat up a little taller and Emmy took notice.

"What?"

"It's the mortgage that's the problem," Jules said. "My parents didn't have to worry about that, and although it's always nice to have extra cash, the clinic is doing really well so I don't actually *need* the money…"

She trailed off, nibbling on her lower lip as she thought. When she didn't continue, Emmy guessed, "You thinking of renting the place?"

"No," Jules said, distracted as the gears turned. "If I rented the house, I'd still have to run the rescue myself." What she really needed was somebody to take the rescue completely off her hands, a person who would care for the rabbits and love the farmhouse as much as her parents had. "But maybe I could give it away – with a contest or something. 'Win a rabbit rescue'."

Emmy laughed. "Who are you, Willy Wonka?"

Jules was too deep inside her own head to laugh with her. "No, but it would be sort of like that. I could vet the applicants, make sure they're up to the task and in it for the right reasons. And I could help them learn the ropes before I step away. Then when I'm sure they're the right person for the job, I can sign the deed over..."

"*Sign* it over?" Emmy asked, narrowly avoiding a spit-take. "You know what this property is worth. The land alone—"

"That's not what matters to me," Jules said, but Emmy's Realtor brain had kicked in and she was salivating over all that lost commission. She barely even heard the rest. "I care way more about making sure the rescue keeps operating, and that it doesn't get dismantled just because some land-hungry developer wants to put up more houses."

"Well, let me know if that's what you decide because I won't waste my time trying to dig up any more leads," Emmy said, suddenly curt as she stood up from the glider.

Jules caught her hand. "Hey."

Their eyes locked and not for the first time, Jules noticed that Emmy was a pretty woman. She always wore heels that accentuated her calves and her lips were always perfectly colored in pink. If it wasn't for their twenty-year age difference – and Emmy's husband – Jules might have made a move.

Instead, she just wanted a little reassurance, and any friend would do.

"What?" Emmy asked.

"Tell me honestly – do you think it's a terrible idea?"

Emmy closed her eyes and made a big show of exhaling, then said, "Every Realtor fiber in my being wants to say yes... but I think your folks would have approved. Promise you won't go off half-cocked – get some legal advice. It might not even be possible."

"Of course," Jules said, letting go of Emmy's hand. "I'll talk to Marissa tomorrow."

As she watched Emmy descend the porch steps and disappear around the side of the house, Jules couldn't help getting hopeful that she might have finally found a solution to her problem.

2

PARKER

ONE MONTH LATER

*P*arker Rose had a lump in her throat.

It had been there for weeks, and in the back of her mind no matter what else she was doing, she was always aware of that lump.

At first, she figured she was coming down with something – she'd gotten strep throat a lot as a kid and she was no stranger to swollen tonsils. But there was no soreness, no icky white patches in the back of her mouth, and she'd even subjected herself to the dreaded throat swab at the doctor's office – which came back clean.

Still, every time she swallowed, there it was – the lump.

Her boyfriend, David, told her it must be allergies.

When she called to talk to her parents on the phone, her mom said she just needed to get out more, get some fresh air. Her dad thought it was all the pollution in Chicago, where Parker and David had moved after high school.

Her best friend, Kani, said it was stress. How convenient was it that this lump appeared just days after David announced that he was officially being considered for partnership at the law firm where he worked? Kani thought it was obvious, but Parker refused to entertain the idea – what kind of terrible girlfriend would react with a physical ailment when her significant other was finally on the verge of achieving the thing he'd been working toward for the last five years?

Parker tried to tell Kani that she was misreading the situation. She was in Helsinki – Parker had met her a couple years ago in an online forum for rabbit lovers – and even though Kani's English was nearly perfect, things did sometimes get lost in translation.

ParksAndWreck: Maybe it's a cultural barrier thing, or maybe it just doesn't translate to text well.

KaniConeja: Or maybe I can see it clearly because I'm about as far from the situation as possible, halfway around the world. You're worried that he's about to get everything he ever wanted and he might not hold up his end of the bargain.

ParksAndWreck: That sounds so selfish.

KaniConeja: You're not the one being selfish.

Parker had been with David ever since they were sixteen years old. She'd never known any other romantic partner – never known any other type of life. For years, she'd put off her own dreams and goals to help David pursue his, and he'd promised that as soon as he made partner, he'd have room in his schedule, his mind, his heart for everything else.

A house outside the crowded city.

A wedding.

Kids, or at the very least, a furry addition to their family.

David was about to get everything he ever dreamed of, but he showed no signs of being ready to start chasing Parker's dreams next. What if it was all a lie?

She'd rather go down WebMD rabbit holes thinking that the lump in her throat was thyroid disease, or even cancer, than believe that he really had been selling her a bill of goods for the last twelve years.

But today was the culmination of a week-long trial for one of the firm's most important clients. The partners had put David in charge of the case and they hadn't said it out loud, but they all knew this was his test – succeed and be promoted to junior partner, fail and keep spinning his wheels as an associate.

He'd made his closing argument today and now all that was left was to wait on the jury. The verdict would seal David's fate just as much as the client's, and Parker's along with it. The lump had been growing bigger and bigger in her throat all day, and she'd come home from her own work at the Humane Society with a bag full of groceries to make him a special dinner.

It was *not* because she felt guilty for questioning his motives. It was just a celebration of a job well done.

While she cooked, Parker had the television on and she kept an eye on the news, hoping to hear something about the trial – the client was a high-ranking CEO for a retail chain based out of downtown Chicago and his embezzlement accusations had turned into a high-profile case over the last few months. It was very unlikely that there'd be a verdict already, but Parker hoped that by the time David came home tonight, he'd be a little more relaxed than he had been over the last few weeks.

Maybe ready to talk about house-hunting, even. They could get a nice place in the suburbs, where Parker could have pets and David could commute into the city for work. She hated the noise and the crowds in Chicago, but David loved it. They'd been here twelve years, ever since college, and he kept promising that someday, she'd have the yard and the space and the bunnies that she wanted.

So she cooked an expensive cut of steak in a cast iron skillet for David, and a Beyond Burger for herself. She'd given up meat around the same time she'd started working at the Humane Society, while David was still in law school, but he'd always refused to take that leap with her.

"Real men eat meat," he'd said the first and only time she'd tried to serve him a veggie burger.

"Real men eat what their girlfriends prepare when they're nice enough to cook them dinner," Parker had said with a cheeky smile. David had choked down the veggie burger, but he wasn't happy about it and he never ate one again.

She didn't buy meat often after that, preferring to order in so she and David could each have what they wanted, but tonight was a special occasion – a celebration. She made garlic mashed potatoes to go along with their entrees and decanted a bottle of red wine to top it all off.

By the time David got home a little after six, everything was ready and laid out on the little dining table that functionally separated the kitchen from the living room in their small, expensive apartment downtown. He dropped his briefcase on the floor near the door and loosened his tie, groaning, "Wow, that smells good."

"I made you a steak," Parker said as David shed articles of clothing.

"Really?" His tie fell to the floor. He kicked off his dress shoes. He draped his suit jacket over the back of the couch.

She nodded. "Yep, medium-rare just how you like it."

He looked exhausted, with faint rings of sweat on his undershirt. He gave her a quick kiss on the cheek and thanked her, then sank down into his chair at the table.

"How did it go?" she asked, sitting next to him.

He sighed as he picked up a steak knife and fork. "Won't know until the jury comes back, but I think we made a good argument. Definitely raised a reasonable doubt, at least in my mind."

He stuffed a big chunk of steak into his cheek and let out a groan of pleasure, and Parker tried not to register her frustration at that answer. He knew that wasn't what she meant – she wanted to know if any of the partners had hinted at their decision. But she didn't want to pester him because she knew he was preoccupied with that too.

While they ate, David asked, "How was your day?"

Parker picked up her burger, wondering if she'd be able to swallow around the lump in her throat.

"Good," she said. "Walked a bunch of dogs. Helped a cute little Himalayan cat get adopted. No new bunnies at the shelter today but I did get two more orders from repeat customers on my Etsy shop."

She'd been running a marginally profitable online business out of the apartment for the last year, making homemade, healthy rabbit treats first for her friends on the forum and then for a larger customer base on Etsy. With low profit margins and sales coming in at a trickle, it was purely a passion project – if she couldn't have pets in the apartment, then at least she could enjoy the pictures of other people's furry family members enjoying her treats.

"That's great," David said. "Repeat business is a good sign. What is that, ten bucks in your pocket?"

Eight, actually, after Etsy takes its cut, she thought. David never did share her passion for animals, and she knew he thought any job that didn't pull in six figures wasn't worth doing, but he tried to be encouraging with what little energy he had left at the end of the day.

"Oh!" Parker said after a few moments of silent chewing, "Did you hear about the contest that's going viral online?"

"Contest?"

"Yeah," Parker said. "Somebody in Ohio is running an essay contest to find a new owner for their rabbit rescue. It comes with a farmhouse and forty acres – it sounds pretty idyllic."

"You found a contest where you can win a rabbit rescue?" David asked, amusement written all over his face. "Only you, Parks."

Parker had a hutch rabbit when she was a kid – a pure white lop named Snowball – and everyone who'd ever laid eyes on her thought she was the cutest stinking thing in existence. Parker always thought she'd get another rabbit someday, when she and David moved out of this apartment and preferably into someplace with a yard, but Parker was twenty-eight years old and *someday* hadn't happened yet.

It was nice working with animals all day, especially when there were rabbits at the shelter – Parker's favorite – but lately, whenever she mentioned her business or Bunny Central, David said he was beginning to think she was obsessed. She could have said the same about his quest to make partner.

"Actually," Parker said, "Kani found it on Bunny Central."

The contest was too good not to mention. She'd been daydreaming about it ever since Kani sent her the link. "Don't you think it could be fun?" Parker pressed. "The rescue is practically self-sufficient so we could essentially live off the land, leave all the stresses of the big city behind. Besides, I really miss small town living. Don't you?"

"No night life, no shopping districts, no high-profile clients?" he said. "No thanks."

Parker and David had grown up rural, with less than fifty students in their graduating class. When he first floated the idea of moving to Chicago for school, Parker had been excited by the idea – the opportunities, the people, the big wide world beyond her small-town life. And living in the city was the only way for David to chase his dream of becoming a big shot trial lawyer.

But Parker always imagined moving back to a small town eventually – or at the very least, the suburbs, where the houses weren't so close together and there wasn't so much light and sound pollution.

"Would it be so bad to go back to a quieter life?" she asked. He was close to achieving his goals – she knew that and she tried to be supportive – but sometimes it felt like David making partner was at the expense of everything else in their lives. "You could be a general practice lawyer—"

"Yeah, sure," he said sarcastically. "Give all this up and breed rabbits just when I'm about to make partner—"

"*Rescue* rabbits," Parker said, but the lump reared its ugly head again, threatening to choke off her words. She was just trying to daydream about a different life – she knew it wasn't real – but he couldn't even play along with her for a couple of minutes.

David was in his element here. He loved the city, loved living downtown and working himself to exhaustion every day for scumbags who stole millions from their companies and then got away with it thanks to his firm. It fueled David, but it was slowly killing Parker.

Their dreams were not the same... not at all.

She set her burger down, untouched. "I don't know if I can do this anymore."

"You want to go back to meat?" David asked.

"No," she said. "I mean *this*."

She gestured around the tiny apartment, at his clothes strewn wherever they fell as he walked in the door, at the ridiculously expensive haircut that David treated himself to once a week. Absolutely none of it felt like it belonged to her. It felt like waking up right in the middle of someone else's life.

And the funny thing was that the moment Parker realized it, the lump in her throat disappeared and she could breathe again. How long had she been bottling all of it up?

"I know this place is kind of cramped," David said, still eating his steak and potatoes. "We'll get a bigger place as soon as they make me a junior partner – it comes with a pretty hefty pay raise. You could have an office for your treat business."

Parker shook her head. "It's not enough. David, none of this is enough for me anymore."

That finally got his attention. He set down his fork and looked at her, confusion across his face. "What does that mean?"

"You were never going to move to the suburbs with me, were you?"

"Parks," he objected, "what's so great about the damn suburbs?"

"It's what *I* want," she said. "We've been together for twelve years and somewhere along the line, you seem to have forgotten – maybe we both have – that I'm here too. I deserve to have my own goals, my own dreams."

"You've got your rabbit treat business," David said, sounding a bit lost and oblivious. "And the shelter – you like your job."

"I do," she agreed, "but I want more than that. Ever since you went to law school, I've been putting off my own dreams while I wait for you to achieve yours, but be honest – making junior partner isn't the end of the climb, is it? You're never going to be happy until you own the whole freaking firm, and you're never going to have the energy to come home at night and help me work on *my* dreams because ultimately, you just think yours are more important than mine."

David sat back in his chair, finally letting her words sink in. Parker had been thinking all of this in the back of her mind for months – maybe even years – but it was all hitting David out of the blue. Except… in his eyes, recognition flickered and she knew he must have sensed on some level that this was coming. They both had.

Finally, after what felt like forever, he crossed his arms defensively over his chest and said, "I never told you to give up on your dreams, Parker."

"I know," she said. "It was my decision to defer them for your sake, but I was young, dumb and in love, and it was a mistake. I can't do it anymore. I'm not happy here,

David. I'm not happy with this life." She contemplated that for a moment, then added, "I think we're holding each other back."

"Shit, Parks," he said. She thought he'd argue, tell her he loved her and that they should figure out a way for them both to be happy. Instead, all he said was, "I think you're right. So what do we do now?"

Ouch.

She thought for a moment and couldn't come up with a single reason to keep treading water with David, so she stood up. "I'm going to call my parents and see if they'll let me come home for a few days because you and I clearly need some space. Then I'm going to figure out what *I* want to do with my life."

"You don't have to leave," he said, standing too but not making any move toward her.

"I don't want to stay," she answered. She figured it would hurt more to break up with the only person she'd ever been with, but the fact that it wasn't harder to walk away must mean that it was time to move on.

She went down the hallway toward the bedroom. About ten minutes later, after she'd talked to her mom and made arrangements to take the bus home to southern Illinois the following day, David appeared in the doorway. He leaned one shoulder against the door jamb and watched while Parker took a weekend's worth of clothes out of her closet.

"What are you gonna do?" he asked. "You're not going to enter that rabbit breeder contest, are you?"

"Rescue," she corrected him. "It's a rescue... and I

don't know. I haven't thought any further than where I'm going to sleep tonight."

"In the bed," David said. "I'll take the couch."

---

*I*n the morning, David was sound asleep on the couch when Parker crept quietly out of the apartment and got into a taxi that would take her to the bus depot.

It was a six-hour bus ride to Mount Vernon, where her parents lived, and Parker sat with her forehead against the cool glass of the window for a couple of hours until it was around 4pm in Helsinki and she knew that Kani would be done with her classes for the day. Then, throwing caution and long-distance rates to the wind, Parker called her. Even though Parker would have plenty of opportunity to talk over everything that had just happened with her parents in a few hours, she really needed a friendly ear right now.

"Parker?" Kani asked as she picked up the phone. She spoke English just as well as she spoke Finnish, but her accent was thick and Parker's name always came out with a slight roll to the Rs.

"I'm glad you picked up," Parker said. "Can you talk?"

"Yes," Kani said. *Yesh*. "Is something wrong?"

"Umm…" Parker wasn't quite sure how to answer that. *Was* there anything wrong? She didn't feel nearly as heartbroken or out of place as she thought she was supposed to after her twelve-year relationship had ended. She decided to stick to the facts. "I broke up with David last night."

"Oh my God," Kani said. "How are you feeling?"

"Surprisingly okay," Parker said. "I left this morning while he was sleeping. I didn't want to have to do the whole *goodbye* thing, and I don't really know how I feel. I love him, or at least I did for a long time, but it just wasn't right anymore. I'm on a bus right now to stay with my parents for the weekend and figure out my next move."

"*Oh my God!*" Kani said, even more animated than before. "Rabbit rescue! That is your next move!"

Parker had to laugh, and she was relieved to find a smile on her lips. Leave it to Kani to immediately zero in on the only thing that could make Parker laugh right now. "I don't know – that seems rash."

"Umm, what better time to do something impulsive than when your life is already changing?" Kani said. "Besides, you're perfect for the job – you work at a shelter and you make cute little treats for bunnies, which my little guys love, by the way. Put me down as a reference – and tell them you are, what did David call you, a rabbit freak?"

"Ugh," Parker groaned. He'd always made it sound like such a bad thing. "I can't just quit my job and move to a new state."

"Why not?" Kani insisted.

Parker didn't have a good answer for that, so she chewed on it for a minute and said, "There are probably far more qualified people entering that contest than me.

I've owned one rabbit in my whole life, and we get them occasionally at the shelter but it's mostly cats and dogs."

"Doesn't matter – it sounds like fate to me," Kani said. Parker laughed again, and at last, Kani let up on her ridiculous idea and said, "So, tell me what happened with David."

Parker relaxed into her seat, settling in for the long drive while she told her friend what happened last night – and in the process, started to work through the years of frustration herself.

3

JULES

TWO MONTHS LATER

"Are you guys ready to meet your new mommy?" Jules asked.

She was in an old pair of her mom's galoshes and she'd just finished mucking out all the rabbit stalls, and now she was transferring some of the bunnies that played well together to a shady outdoor run so they could get some exercise.

A brindle-patterned orange and black rabbit named Murphy hopped to the front of his stall as Jules passed with Cotton in her arms. The look in Murphy's eyes was clear – *can I come too?*

"You work on not biting so much, Murph," Jules said. "Then we can talk about group playtime. And maybe apologize to Buttons – she's still missing a tuft of fur from her backside."

It was exhausting trying to make sure every one of the nearly two dozen bunnies currently at the rescue got equal playtime, and that no one who was enemies with anyone else accidentally got put in the run together.

It was a full-time job for sure, and Jules had been doing that *plus* running her veterinary practice for the last ten months. It was high time for someone else to take over, and that someone was scheduled to arrive today. Jules was excited, and she was pretty sure the rabbits could sense it – they were all full of energy today too.

She put Cotton down inside the run and the little white rabbit immediately kicked her back feet up, flipping in the air in an exuberant leap before joining the others. Then Jules checked her watch.

Twelve-thirty. Her contest winner would be here in about half an hour and Jules had the place exactly as she wanted it – clean and orderly, with a bunch of adorable bunnies running around to immediately make the new rescue owner fall in love.

Well, almost-owner.

Marissa, the estate attorney, had smartly built a trial period of twelve weeks into the terms of the contest. That way the winner could learn whatever they needed from Jules, and Jules could make sure they were really up to the task of running the rescue.

Jules had designed the contest to be quick and simple. *Write an essay explaining why you're the right person to inherit my family's rabbit rescue, and the winner gets a fully operational rescue complete with bunnies, a house and forty acres.*

But she'd underestimated what the response would be like. Over five thousand applicants submitted essays in the thirty days the contest was open, and it hadn't taken Jules long to see from the range of submissions that Marissa's idea was a good one. Some entries were good – impressive, even – and others seemed half-hearted at best. And Jules had to make sure that whoever she picked was really right for the job – not just a good essayist.

Still, she hoped the winner she'd chosen – a woman colorfully named Parker Rose – would be a quick learner, highly motivated and an independent type.

It was almost exactly one o'clock when Jules heard tires crunching over the gravel and she came around the side of the barn, nibbling on her lip and feeling a little more anxious than she expected to.

It made sense, though – she was about to hand over her parents' property. She'd lived here her whole life and the rescue had been a huge part of her childhood. Her parents' love for animals was what inspired her to become a vet, and even though she wouldn't officially sign the property over to Parker for three more months, if all went well, it was suddenly feeling rather final.

That's what you wanted, she reminded herself as a rusty little Geo came to a stop in front of the house. Too late, she realized she was still wearing her mom's muddy galoshes and her black T-shirt was covered in fur. Cotton never seemed to stop shedding.

But there was nothing Jules could do about that, and

any true rabbit lover wouldn't think twice about a little stray fur and some mud, anyway.

The car door opened and a tall brunette stepped out. It was almost comical how much taller she was than the tiny car, but as soon as she closed the door, Jules forgot all about that and tried not to notice how attractive the woman was. She had long, straight hair that fell over her shoulders. She wore a baby blue sundress that just brushed the middle of her thighs, and the moment her eyes locked onto Jules, she smiled warmly.

Jules bit her lip a little bit harder. She always did have a weakness for brunettes.

Stop, she commanded herself. *You cannot be attracted to your contest winner.*

She could already hear Marissa's objections to the legal complications that would be introduced if Jules made a move on this woman. It was best to just put that thought completely out of her head and never go there again.

She crossed the yard, holding out her hand. "Hi, I'm Jules Wakefield. You must be Parker."

The woman took her hand and Jules noticed her nails – short but very neatly manicured. *We'll see how long those last out here,* she thought.

"I am," she confirmed. "It's nice to meet you."

Her eyes were even prettier up close, picking up the hues of her dress as they swept over the farm and tried to take everything in. She looked enthusiastic, if a bit overwhelmed, but Jules figured she'd probably feel that way herself if she'd been living in a high-rise in downtown

Chicago a couple months ago and suddenly found herself the sole proprietor of a rabbit rescue in the middle of Ohio farm country.

She knew all of that from Parker's essay, and she also hoped that this girl really did have the mix of compassion, entrepreneurial spirit and responsibility that Jules had been looking for. She'd said all the right things in her contest entry, in any case.

"Do you want to come around to the porch and sit down a minute, have a bottle of water or a soda?" Jules asked. "You must be exhausted from the drive."

"That would be great, actually," Parker said, giving Jules a shy smile and stirring something desirous in her belly that she tried hard to quash. "My car doesn't have air conditioning."

Jules' eyes widened. "It's almost ninety degrees out today. And you drove all the way from Illinois, is that right?"

Parker nodded. "Yep, but it was worth it – I want you to know how much it means that you chose me. The truth is that I had to sell some things just to buy that car and get down here, but I want you to know I'm fully committed to running the rescue just like your parents always did."

Jules gave her a strained smile. She'd included as little background information as she could get away with on the contest website, only revealing that the rescue had been in her family for twenty years, that her parents had passed last September and it was important to her that their legacy be preserved... but those were all the details she could bring herself to include. She hoped Parker wouldn't ask for more.

"I'm glad you're here," she said. "Come on, I'll get you that water."

She led Parker around the side of the house and up the steps to the covered porch, and while she retrieved a couple bottles of water from the mini-fridge, Parker stood near the screen and looked out at the rabbit run in the shade of the barn.

Jules watched her for a moment, her eyes dipping down to the curves just beneath the thin fabric of Parker's sundress before coming back up to her face. She was grinning, completely unselfconscious, as she watched the rabbits leap and play. It was a good sign.

Jules knew that Parker's personal experience with rabbits was limited – just one pet when she was a girl and the occasional rabbit at the Humane Society – but compassion and a willingness to learn mattered more to her than a long résumé, and Parker was positively glowing with excitement.

Jules took a quick moment to try and brush the biggest tufts of Cotton's fur off her shirt, then came to Parker's side. She nudged Parker's arm and handed her one of the water bottles, and Parker looked a little bashful, caught in an unguarded moment. "They're really cute."

"They're all yours," Jules said. "Well, at least until you're able to find them permanent homes, anyway."

"Are there a lot of people in Camden who want rabbits as pets?" Parker asked. "I did a little research into the town and the population is pretty small. Just over ten thousand?"

"Sounds about right," Jules said. "My parents placed a few rabbits with families in Camden every year, but mostly people come from the surrounding areas to adopt the bunnies. My mom and dad did a lot of legwork to make sure people from nearby counties knew about the rescue – adoption events, a Facebook page, stuff like that. But I can teach you all about that – there's plenty of time."

"Good," Parker said. She took a long pull from the water bottle, then said, "I'm sorry for your loss. It must have been very hard."

"It still is," Jules admitted. And then, because she didn't want to dwell on the subject any longer than necessary, she said, "So tell me about yourself – I mean, whatever you couldn't fit into a one-page essay. What turned you into a 'bunny freak'?"

Parker laughed. "Well, I don't know if I'd say *freak*, although my ex was partial to that term."

She looked down at her shoes, a pair of canvas sneakers already dusty from the gravel driveway. She seemed guarded now, and it reminded Jules a little bit of how some of the rabbits who came through the rescue acted when they first arrived – skittish and untrusting. It always broke Jules' heart, and she had the urge to wrap her arms around Parker now.

Parker said, "I had a rabbit when I was a kid – Snowball. She stole my heart... she was the sweetest little thing and she always loved me, was always happy to see me no matter what. I wanted to get another rabbit after my boyfriend, David, and I got settled in Chicago, but we were in a small apartment. That's no place for a house rabbit."

The mention of a male ex did not escape Jules' notice. Good to know – now maybe she could stop admiring Parker's eyes, and those impossibly long legs.

"Anyway," Parker said, brightening, "I never stopped wanting a pet the whole time I lived in the city so I spent a lot of time on Bunny Central – do you know that forum?"

Jules nodded. It was the largest rabbit-focused forum on the internet and it had an adoption sub-forum that her parents made use of.

"I made some friends there and a couple times, I made homemade treats for special occasions and shipped them out. The rabbits loved them and their owners shared pictures all around the forum, and pretty soon I started getting requests. My best friend told me I'd be a fool not to charge for them, at least to recoup my expenses, and that's how I ended up with a gourmet rabbit treat business, The Happy House Rabbit," Parker said. "Making the treats is fun, but seeing all the pictures of bunnies enjoying my creations is what I really like. It's the next best thing to having one of my own... but of course you know all that from, uh, my essay."

She tripped over the end of that sentence and Jules wondered if there was more to the story. Did something bad happen with the ex? Was it an ugly break-up?

It's none of your business, Jules reminded herself.

Parker was here to do a job – not tell Jules all the intimate details of her past.

"Well," she said, slapping her thighs, "You've got about two dozen of them now. I bet you want to meet them, and I need to make sure they're getting enough shade. Or, well, I guess *you* need to do that. This place is yours now, after all."

For the next two hours, Jules showed Parker everything she needed to know – at least for starters. They met the rabbits and toured the property, and Parker whipped a little notepad out of her back pocket and took frenzied notes on pretty much everything that came out of Jules' mouth.

"And where do you get the lettuce from?" Parker asked as Jules was showing her around the barn.

"From the garden," Jules said. "We grow them here – cuts down on costs."

Parker frowned. "I don't have much of a green thumb, but I'll do the best I can."

"You'll learn as you go," Jules said. "The margins around here are pretty tight so I wouldn't recommend buying lettuce for two dozen rabbits in town, but if you have to do it until you get the hang of gardening, it's not the end of the world."

"Maybe..." Parker started to say, then looked down at her notepad.

"What?"

"I don't want to be a nuisance, but do you think you could come over sometime and give me a gardening tutorial?"

It looked like it physically pained her to ask for that extra help, which should have thrilled Jules – she was looking for someone who would take direction and help lighten her load, not someone who was going to need their hand held for the next three months. But she got the impression that Parker needed to feel self-sufficient.

"Of course—" she started to say.

"I mean, I know you have a lot on your plate," Parker added.

"It's okay."

"I'll be a quick study." She was trying so hard to reassure Jules, to keep from being a burden. Again, Jules had the urge to put her arms around Parker. She got the distinct impression that nobody had ever done that for her before — stood by her, supported her like she deserved.

"Seriously, it's fine," Jules tried to reassure her. "I've been tending that garden since I was a teenager – I'd be happy to show you what I know."

Parker smiled, and her shoulders relaxed out of the defensive posture she'd unconsciously raised them into. Jules kept showing her around and Parker took so many notes Jules thought she might run out of room on her notepad.

At last, Jules steeled herself and took Parker on a tour of the house. She'd gone inside twice recently – once a week ago to dust and stash away some of the 'knickknacks and clutter' that might get in Parker's way – and again this morning to drop off a bag of staple groceries from her favorite mom-and-pop market in town so that Parker wouldn't arrive to a barren pantry.

The first time was hard. The second time was a little easier. And now that Parker was here, distracting Jules with her studious little notebook and cute look of determination, Jules found it was hardly difficult at all to step over the threshold. Still, she kept the tour brief and encouraged Parker to explore on her own, then led her back outside.

They went around to the outdoor run, where it was time to give a new set of rabbits exercise, and watching Parker bond with the bunnies turned out to be the best part of the afternoon, hands down.

The very first thing she did when they got to the run was drop to her knees and stick her fingers through the wire mesh so Jack, the little lionhead, could sniff at her. He did, then lost interest and hopped away, and when Parker looked up at Jules, there was a massive smile on her face.

Jules couldn't help laughing. "Jack's a real ladies' man. He has that effect on a lot of women."

"I didn't realize how much I missed having bunnies in my life," Parker said. "I always had fun with the shelter rabbits, but I didn't get to really bond with them because our first priority was always getting them adopted as quickly as possible so they wouldn't have to sit there and listen to dogs barking around the clock. These ones... I'm going to really get to know them, aren't I?"

"You can go in there with them," Jules said, pointing to the gate on the side of the run.

"Really?"

Jules laughed again. "Just try not to fall in love. Makes it harder to find homes for them if you get attached."

She knew that fact well. How many rabbits had come through the rescue over the years and wound up inside the farmhouse instead of being adopted? Dozens – and her dad always seemed to be the one sneaking them into the house, making up stories about how this rabbit didn't like the barn, or that rabbit didn't get along with the others. Once they came inside the house, they were part of the family.

Jules hadn't had a pet of her own since before her parents passed. At first it was too difficult, trying to juggle the vet clinic and her family and social life, and then her mother's quick and brutal illness. And then after they died, she found that she didn't have the time *or* the heart for it.

She held out her hand and helped Parker up, then led the way over to the gate. She stepped inside and Jules closed the gate again quickly to keep any escape artists from pulling a Houdini, and then Jules watched Parker get down on her knees again, not minding that she was getting dirty as she held out her hands and let the bunnies come up to her.

While Parker was occupied with them, Jules went into the barn to get a few fresh carrots that she'd dug out of the garden earlier in the day. When she came back,

Parker already had Jack on her lap and Cotton marking the heel of her sneaker as her property.

Jules rested her forearms on top of the gate, watching Parker laugh and grin as more and more rabbits surrounded her. The sun beat down on her dark hair, making it shimmer in the light, and there was pure happiness in the expression on her face.

She might not have a green thumb, or a ton of experience with rabbits, but it seemed like she needed this place, and the rabbits obviously loved her already, even without the carrots Jules had fetched to bribe them.

"You're a natural," she said, opening the gate softly to join her.

"They're so cute, I don't know how I'll ever part with any of them," Parker said.

Jules laughed and sat down beside her, then handed her a carrot. "Here – I'm sure it doesn't hold a candle to your treats, but these rabbits like carrots well enough." While they passed out treats, creating a furry little feeding frenzy around them, she added, "Be careful with that attitude, by the way. The barn holds fifty but let me tell you from personal experience, you do *not* want fifty rabbits. It'll be nothing but little poops everywhere, as far as the eye can see."

Parker laughed too, maybe at what Jules had said or maybe because they both had rabbits literally crawling over their laps to get to the carrots.

When they ran out, Jules stood up and held out her hand to Parker again, pulling her to her feet. They stood close to each other for just a beat – close enough to see little gray flecks in Parker's blue eyes, close enough to kiss her coral-painted lips. And then Jules let go of her hand and said, "Come on, help me get these guys back in the barn and I'll introduce you to the rest of them. And remind me before I leave tonight – I'll give you the number for the vet clinic, as well as my cell in case you need me."

4
PARKER

Parker woke out of a dead sleep to the sound of her phone vibrating insistently right beside her head.

"Unh!" She grunted, disoriented as she reached blindly in the direction of the noise. It was dark outside the windows of the unfamiliar bedroom and her first thought was that it must be Kani calling from the other side of the world. It would be unusual of her, but not totally out of character, to forget about the time difference if she had something urgent to say. She was a student, which meant she sometimes kept unusual hours anyway.

But when Parker's hand finally found her phone and she sat up in bed, she saw that it was a quarter to six in the morning and *Mom* flashed across the screen.

Parker answered, her heart climbing into her throat. "Mom? What's going on? Is everything okay?"

Her parents were in their sixties, retired, and other

than the usual complaints of old age, they were both in good health. But that didn't stop Parker from imagining the worst when her mother called in what felt like the middle of the night.

"Everything's fine on our end," her mom said, and the calmness of her voice was reassuring.

Parker flopped back against the headboard, letting out a relieved sigh as she asked, "Did you have to call before sunrise in that case?"

"Yes," her mom said, "because you promised to call when you got to Ohio, but we never heard a thing! Here I was picturing you broken down on the side of the road, or abducted and chained to a radiator in some serial killer's house."

"Shit," Parker muttered to herself. She did forget to call, but she couldn't help chuckling at where her mom's mind went. "You watch too many true crime shows."

"It's not funny!" her mom objected.

"Do you think there are many serial killers in rural Ohio?" Parker teased.

"I don't know," her mom said, defensive. "The good ones don't get caught."

True enough, Parker thought. "Mom, I'm sorry I forgot to call. The drive was exhausting, and then I spent the whole afternoon with the rescue owner going over everything..."

Jules' face floated into Parker's mind. Her cheekbone-length hair was forever falling in her eyes, she didn't need a stitch of makeup over her flawless skin, and she seemed completely comfortable tromping around the property in a pair of muddy rain boots all day. The phrase *salt of the earth* came to mind, and so did *country girl*. Jules reminded Parker of a lot of the people she went to high school with, and she'd felt immediately at ease with her.

"...I had to feed and exercise the bunnies," she went on, "and it was nine p.m. before I even came inside the house. I wouldn't even have eaten dinner last night if Jules hadn't thought to leave me some groceries."

She knew even as she said it that this information would not help her mother relax about the idea of her only child living alone on a farm in another state. But it was a curious thing – as soon as Parker stepped out from behind the wheel of the Geo she knew she was home.

Her mom let out a sigh right into the phone. "Oh, doodlebug, that sounds like a lot to handle all by yourself. And you're going to need treat supplies so you can make money—"

"Mom," Parker cut her off, trying to sound casual. "I'll find a grocery store today and get everything I need – promise."

She was doing her best to reassure her mom. Despite the fact that she'd left most of her belongings in Chicago when she decided not to return to the city, and she only had $500 left in her pocket after buying the car, Parker really wasn't worried about getting supplies right now, or whether she'd be able to keep the rescue running smoothly.

She'd survived one crisis – the abrupt end of a twelve-year relationship – and landed on her feet. It was scary as hell, and she'd had her doubts the whole time, but she just kept pushing forward and so far, she hadn't fallen flat on her face.

"You've never done anything like this before," her mom said, giving voice to all the unspoken concerns that Parker had been trying hard to push aside.

"Thanks for the reminder."

She was right. Parker had never lived alone before. She'd gone straight from her parents' house to a dorm room in Chicago while she and David were in college, and then to that small, expensive apartment. Then back to her parents' house for a few months when she needed a soft place to land.

And now she was on her own, in a huge, unfamiliar house that made strange noises in the night, with almost two dozen rabbits in the barn outside. She didn't know how to run a rabbit rescue, she didn't know how to be by herself... hell, she hadn't even entered that contest.

Kani had written the essay and entered it in Parker's name after Parker had realized she couldn't afford to go back to Chicago and get an apartment of her own just to keep working at a non-profit shelter that paid her minimum wage. She had her treat business, which barely helped cover the cost of the food she was eating out of her parents' kitchen, and she knew she had to find a job and start helping out financially if she was going to stay in Mount Vernon.

Kani didn't confess until the day Parker received a very bewildering, congratulatory email from a woman named Jules Wakefield, and by then she'd already discovered that there were no jobs to be had in her tiny, depressed hometown in southern Illinois. It seemed better to take the chance and chase a dream rather than come clean about what Kani had done.

Parker still wasn't sure how she felt about all that. She wasn't a liar, but Kani had written that essay to make Parker's dream come true, and it was too tempting to pass up.

And Jules... Parker wasn't sure how she felt about her yet, either. There was something deeply sad about her – it was obvious as soon as they met that she was still mourning the deaths of her parents, and that being on the property was painful for her. But at the same time, Parker could tell Jules had a big heart. She may not want to show it off, but she cared deeply about the rabbits, and about the rescue.

Jules had explained how the rescue and her vet clinic worked together, checking the health of all the new arrivals and doing free spaying and neutering before the rabbits were adopted in exchange for referrals back to the clinic.

There was no way that was a fair arrangement – maybe it made sense when the rescue was a family business, but Parker was a stranger and as soon as she heard it, she was determined to find a way to pay Jules for her veterinary services just as soon as she found her bearings here.

"I'm just saying," her mom continued on the phone, "you can come home anytime you want."

"You sure can," a second voice chimed in, and Parker had to choke back homesick tears.

"Dad, you're up at this ungodly hour too?"

"Newspaper's not gonna read itself," he said. "And hey, you're a farmer now – you better get used to these hours."

Parker laughed. "It's a rabbit rescue, not a farm. It's not like they need to be milked first thing in the morning."

"Now that'd be a sight!" her dad said. "It's good to hear your voice, bug. You doing okay?"

"Yeah, I'm just fine," Parker said. *Just suffering an almost unbearable wave of homesickness,* she thought. She'd forgotten how much she liked living with her parents. It had been nice staying with them for the last couple of months.

"Good to hear it," her dad said. "Anyway, I'll give you back to your mom."

She heard a little bit of shuffling, and then her mom's voice came again. "Parker?"

"I'm here."

"And so are we if you need us," she said.

"Thank you," Parker said.

She knew they meant it – her parents were amazing, generous people. She'd actually seen her father give someone the shirt off his back once, when she was a kid and they'd come across a homeless man begging on the streets. It was summer and the sun was beating down, burning the man's shoulders, so Parker's dad gave the man his T-shirt, along with twenty dollars for a good meal.

And that was exactly why she couldn't go back home

again. It had been enough of a strain on them to feed and shelter her for the last two months while she figured out her next move. They couldn't afford to support her on their retirement income, even though they'd never say so.

Winning Jules' contest – even if Parker'd had no actual part in it – was the best chance she had at building a future for herself and she needed to make it work.

"I'll be okay," she insisted. "The owner, Jules, is really great. She's going to help me get my bearings."

Parker had plans to see Jules the next day so she could learn how *not* to kill everything growing in the garden, and she was already looking forward to it. If she could get the hang of gardening, she'd not only be able to keep the rescue sustainable, but she could increase the profit margin on her treats by growing some of the ingredients. Besides, there was something comforting and familiar about Jules. Parker liked spending time with her.

"Good," her mom said. "Well, once you get settled, we'll have to come out and see the place."

"I'd like that," Parker said, and then her mom said she had to get breakfast started.

"You know how your father gets when he doesn't start the day with some protein," she said, then stage whispered into the phone, *"Bitchy."*

Parker heard her dad register an objection in the background. She laughed and said goodbye, and by the time she hung up the phone, some pre-dawn light was beginning to filter through the window.

The bedroom she'd chosen appeared to have been a guest room in another life. She didn't feel right taking over Jules' parents' bedroom, and for some reason, the idea of sleeping in what had been Jules' bed made Parker blush.

It was always a little uncomfortable to wake up in a room that wasn't familiar, and Parker had felt out of place when she was walking through the big farmhouse all by herself last night. But by the light of day, the place didn't seem quite so daunting anymore.

It was hers – or at least it would be in twelve weeks if all went well – and if she was going to stay there, she'd have to stop thinking of it as 'Jules' parents' house' sooner or later. Still, she could do with a bit more noise – Camden wasn't like downtown Chicago, where city noises could be heard incessantly in the background all the time. Car alarms, sirens, buskers, loud conversations on the sidewalk...

Out here, there was no light pollution or city sounds. It was silent... peaceful... lonely.

Parker tossed the sheets away and got out of bed. She was up so she might as well start her day.

The list of daily chores that Jules had walked Parker through the day before took a few hours, but thanks to the early start, she was done with everything by noon except for giving the bunnies their daily exercise.

For that, she'd have to consult the complicated notes she'd taken – who got along with whom, who should never be allowed to run free together for fighting or *other* F-word reasons.

There were a couple of unaltered rabbits in the barn that couldn't yet mingle with the opposite sex, including one, a black and white Dutch bunny named Buck, who Jules had informed Parker had a neutering appointment later in the week.

That was on the calendar in her phone, along with a couple of adoption events Jules had told her about around the county and one adoption appointment that Jules had set up through Facebook and offered to walk Parker through.

The only thing Parker didn't need a long list of notes on was how to actually identify all those bunnies. She'd noticed all the handwritten name tags hanging on the fronts of the stalls yesterday and asked Jules about it. Jules got embarrassed, saying it was just a habit she'd started when she was a kid and couldn't seem to break.

Parker lingered over the name tags now, looking each one over. They were all unique, the artwork on most of them matching the corresponding rabbit's name. This was not the habitual work of someone who didn't care. It was loving, and it made Parker's chest swell with happiness.

What it took to get here had broken her heart, but now that she had arrived, she could see this was exactly what she'd always wanted.

By the time all the rabbits were fed and happily munching away on home-grown hay, Parker was exhausted and content.

"What's next?" she mused aloud, looking at the time. The afternoon stretched before her and Jules wouldn't be there to give her a gardening lesson for hours. "Give me just a few minutes, okay guys? Gotta get some water."

She went inside the house and headed for the kitchen sink, drinking well water straight from the tap. She'd never quite gotten used to the chemical taste of city water, and she chugged a whole glass before sitting down at the little round table in the corner of the kitchen to review her notes. What other chores could she do today?

It wasn't until the moment her butt hit the chair that she realized how tired she was. Her thighs ached, her tank top stuck to her back from the hot July sun, and it felt like she'd already done a full day's work. She fanned herself for a minute or two, trying to cool down, and she looked around the kitchen.

There were older appliances, circa the 1980s, and the oak table she was sitting at was older too, but everything looked meticulously taken care of – well-loved, as some might call it. And the room was cozily decorated with the requisite gingham curtains tied back against the window above the sink and a matching set of dish towels hanging off the front of the oven.

The whole house was like that – cozy and lived-in but tidy. Parker knew that Jules' parents had both died within a short time of each other, but she didn't know any more details than that. Even though she'd never met them, Parker could tell a lot about their personalities from the house itself, and from the fact that they'd dedicated their lives to improving the lot of rescue rabbits. Jules' parents must have been warm, charitable people, probably a lot like Parker's own parents.

What must it feel like to give her childhood home to a stranger, to trust that person to carry on her parents' work?

She was mulling that over, trying to imagine herself in Jules' shoes, when her phone started to vibrate in the pocket of her shorts. Her first thought was that maybe her mom had thought of something new to worry about, but when she looked at her phone, she saw her best friend's name on the screen. Parker couldn't pick up fast enough.

"Kani!"

"You're keeping me in suspense, woman," Kani said. "You've been there what, two days? And no calls, no texts, *no adorable rabbit photos?!*"

"Twenty-four hours," Parker corrected, quickly doing the mental math and concluding it was around seven p.m. in Finland. "And I'm sorry – I've just been really busy. But I have pictures!"

She'd taken about a hundred of them between last night and this morning's play sessions, mostly because the rabbits were too adorable for words but also because she remembered what Jules had said about the rescue's Facebook page drawing prospective adopters. Parker switched Kani over to speakerphone while she sorted through her camera roll and sent her a few of the best shots.

"Check your texts," she said, then waited.

A few moments later, Kani squealed into the phone so loudly Parker winced. "Oh my God, I want her! What's her name?"

Parker laughed. "Which one? The white one, or the little brindle—"

"The Lionhead!" Kani said. "You know how much I love their squishy little faces."

"That would be Jack," Parker said. "He's a boy and I'm told he's quite the ladies' man."

"Well, shoot. Do you think he'd be competition in that case?" Kani asked. "Or would he make a good wingman?"

Parker smiled. "I bet he could help you pick up chicks. He climbed right into my lap yesterday for a carrot."

"How does he feel about international travel?" Kani asked. "And does he get along with other boys?"

Kani had five rabbits of her own – three Flemish giants all from the same litter and two rescues she'd taken in from friends. And until a very short time ago, Parker thought Kani was crazy to keep five rabbits at once. Now she had roughly two dozen of her own.

"I haven't gotten to know him well enough to judge," Parker said. "But if you're serious—"

Kani let out a long, disappointed sigh. "No, it would be cruel to put him on an airplane. He'll just have to find a local family. Boy, Parker, I don't know how you're going to do it – I could never give any of them away."

Parker smiled. "That's what I told Jules yesterday."

"Ah, the mysterious benefactor," Kani said. "What's she like?"

"She's great," Parker said. "She runs a veterinary practice in town, she knows everything there is to know about running the rescue, farming, rabbits in general... basically everything I *don't* know. And she's really sweet."

"Sweet?"

"Yeah."

"How so?"

Suddenly Parker's cheeks were burning again. "I don't know. Sweet. She spent the whole afternoon yesterday walking me through every little detail about the rescue, and she's coming over again tonight for more of the same."

"What's she look like?"

"Huh?" Parker asked. "What's that got to do with anything?"

"I don't know," Kani said, playing coy. Parker could practically hear her smiling through the phone. "Your voice just took on this kind of... dreamy quality. I've never heard you sound like that before so I thought maybe she was cute."

Parker was stunned into silence for a moment, then she said, "Umm, I'm straight. Did you forget that?"

"I don't know about that," Kani said. "I have a sixth sense about these things."

"Yeah, I know," Parker said, rolling her eyes. "You've mentioned it a time or two."

"No, *you've* mentioned it," Kani said. "Unless you forgot New Year's Eve?"

Now Parker's cheeks were really burning and she was glad this wasn't a video call. "I was drunk."

"Yes, and *a drunk mind speaks a sober heart*," Kani said.

She was referring to an incident that had taken place two years ago. David had dragged her to a party with a bunch of lawyers he was hoping to rub elbows with, and while he was off schmoozing, Parker spent the whole night talking to an attractive, somewhat androgynous cater-waiter with warm brown eyes.

At midnight, David was nowhere to be found and the girl surprised Parker by pulling her into a quick but deep kiss. The party ended shortly after, Parker never saw the girl again, and when she'd called Kani later to wish her a happy new year, all the details of the kiss had spilled out of her mouth.

David never found out because he'd passed out drunk in bed by then and Kani convinced Parker not to tell him. It was just a little new year's kiss, and yet she never missed an opportunity to bring it up.

"She kissed me," Parker objected now.

"But you *liiiiked* it," Kani said. "All I'm saying is that having a long-term boyfriend doesn't mean you can't switch teams now that you're a free agent again."

Parker laughed. "You've been studying up on American sports terms?"

"I met a girl online and we've been talking," Kani said. "She's a Phillies fan. Anyway, you didn't answer the question. Jules – is she androgynous like your waiter?"

"Oh my God, stop," Parker said. "Even if I liked girls *and* her, *and* she also liked girls, it would never happen.

Eventually I'm going to have to come clean about the essay and she'll probably end up hating me."

"Do *not* tell her," Kani said. "What's done is done."

"No, it's not," Parker argued back. She'd been scolding Kani over submitting that essay for weeks and she'd yet to convince her that it was a serious problem. "You know there's a three-month trial period and if Jules finds out I'm here under false pretenses, she could disqualify me. Then I'll have nowhere to go except back home to be a burden to my parents."

"Relax," Kani said, and Parker wished she could be as casual about the whole thing as her best friend was. It was easy not to be invested when you were on another continent, and Kani was seven years younger than her. Nothing is a big deal when you're twenty-one. "The essay was still *about* you – nothing I put in it was a lie, was it?"

Parker reluctantly agreed. Kani had given her a copy of it after Parker found out what she'd done, and she had to admit it was a good essay, all about how she'd found a creative way to express her passion for rabbits through her business despite living in a situation where she couldn't have any pets of her own. There had been a lot of heart in that essay, and Parker had to reluctantly give Kani credit – she'd been dishonest and sneaky, but she'd done it so that Parker could have a shot at a future that would really make her happy.

"Don't worry," Kani insisted. "It's not like she's going to spend three months training you on how to run the rescue and then throw all that away on a technicality."

Parker thought it was more than a technicality, but she could also see they weren't going to make any headway on that subject. She got up from the kitchen table and wandered into the living room with the phone in her hand. She hadn't taken much time to explore the house last night and she looked around now, describing what she saw to Kani.

"The house is really beautiful," she said. "There are family portraits all over the walls. I'll have to box them up for Jules – I'm sure she'll want to hold onto them."

"She didn't take them already?" Kani asked.

"I think she's having a really hard time with the grieving process," Parker said. "She barely talked about it yesterday, but from what little she did say, I got the impression that she's been trying to ignore her parents' deaths as much as possible."

"That's a shame," Kani said.

"It's a little bit like living in a museum," Parker said as her eyes swept over the living room. "I wouldn't want to change anything because it doesn't feel like it's my place. Oh my God."

"What?"

"I don't think there's a TV," Parker said.

There was a table along one wall, where a TV ordinarily would go, but it only held a lamp. Parker looked around and there were no large cabinets, no entertainment centers where a TV could be hiding. She knew from Jules' tour yesterday that the basement was unfinished, turned into a workshop by her father, and Parker didn't remember seeing a TV in any of the bedrooms either.

"I think you'll live," Kani said.

"I know it's a silly thing to complain about," Parker said. "But I like the background noise. I've never lived alone, and this house is so big and empty."

It hadn't bothered her last night because she'd practically fallen into bed with exhaustion, but the prospect of an entire night of eerie silence unnerved her.

"You don't need TV," Kani said. "You have rabbits to entertain you now."

"During the day, sure," Parker said. "I've got enough chores to keep me busy for hours. But what about at night, when they're in the barn and I'm all alone in this big house?"

"Umm, bring them into the house?"

Parker was dumbstruck for a second or two. She'd been contemplating driving into Camden that afternoon and spending some of her precious savings on a thrift store television, along with groceries, and what Kani suggested hadn't even occurred to her. It seemed beautifully simplistic.

"Am I allowed to do that?"

Kani laughed. "Last I heard, you ran the place. I think you can do whatever you want."

"Wow," she said, the fear subsiding. "Okay, thanks for talking me off that ledge. I feel better."

"What are best friends for?" Kani asked.

When Parker hung up a few minutes later, she was strategizing. She'd have to buy an indoor pen so the rabbits didn't destroy everything in the house, but she had plenty of company just a few yards away in the barn. Besides, she was trying to socialize these rabbits and make them into good pets for their future owners – it made perfect sense to bring them inside.

Thank you, Kani, she thought, and as she headed back outside to finish setting up playtime in the outdoor run, she couldn't help thinking about the wild conclusions Kani had jumped to regarding Jules.

You kiss one random waiter while you're drunk and all of a sudden everyone's questioning your sexuality...

5
JULES

Realistic or not, what Jules had imagined when she sat down to draft the rules of the essay contest had been something along the lines of: Stranger comes to town and Jules spends a few hours a week training them in how to run the rescue. Stranger then takes over and does whatever he, she or they want, except for changing the name. Stranger calls every once in a while with questions, but otherwise works autonomously and Jules goes back to focusing on her veterinary practice, and magically, all her grief and heartache disappears along with her duties at the rescue.

She knew it wouldn't go like that as soon as she chose Parker – first because she was a city girl with a cute little rabbit treat business and second, because she had very little specifically rabbit-related experience. Jules had stealthily ordered a batch of treats before making her final decision and all the rescue rabbits loved them, so she knew Parker was competent at least, but she also knew there'd be a certain amount of hand-holding over the next three months.

What she didn't expect was to enjoy it as much as she did.

Jules went over to the property on Parker's second day and spent a lot more time there than she'd originally planned, teaching her all about gardening. They got down on their hands and knees in the dry, warm soil together and Jules showed Parker the damage an aphid could do to lettuce, how to tell when the carrots were ready, and how much water everything needed.

They worked shoulder-to-shoulder spraying the garden down with an all-natural pest repellent mix that Jules' mom had come up with, and she asked Parker how The Happy House Rabbit was weathering the change in location.

"It's not, at the moment," Parker said. "I had to put the shop in vacation mode for a couple of weeks while I moved and got settled. Oh, and I was wondering if you could point me in the direction of a store where I can buy my ingredients, and maybe also an indoor pen?"

Jules grinned at her. "Have you decided to keep one of them already?"

"No," Parker said, explaining how she wanted to rotate all the bunnies through the house in the evenings to make sure they were friendly and properly socialized.

Jules stood, brushing dirt from her bare knees, and pulled Parker to her feet. "I think that's a great idea. Come on – you can follow me into town and I'll show you where the feed and grain store is, and the grocery store. And let me know if there's anything I can do to help you get your treat business back up to speed. That was a large part of the reason I chose you – because you've got your own way of earning money – but it's not going to do either of us any good if you get overwhelmed right from the start and go broke."

"Thanks," Parker said, relief registering in her eyes. "I am getting kind of hungry to reopen the shop."

"I'm sure your customers are, too." She smiled, wondering whether Parker recognized the Camden address when her order had come in. The rabbits had gone wild for the treats, but if Parker knew Jules had been scoping her out, she hadn't mentioned it yet.

The two of them caravanned the five miles into Camden and parked outside the feed and grain store. Jules got out of her truck and gave Parker directions to a few more vital landmarks – the grocery store, post office, library, and her veterinary office not far from the feed and grain.

"I'll have to go for a drive some evening before it gets dark and see what else Camden has to offer," Parker said, looking around.

"An Amazon Fulfillment Center, soon enough," Jules said, then had to resist cringing at her own words. When had she become like all the real estate agents in the area, focused on the big business taking over her little town?

"Nice," Parker said, raising her eyebrows and pretending to be impressed. God, she was cute, even when she was being sarcastic.

Jules took a step backward, away from Parker's car,

and waved goodbye. She climbed back into her truck just as Parker was heading into the feed and grain, and resisted the urge to watch her walk away in a pair of deliciously short cut-offs.

Jules focused on her work for the next couple of days, fielding the odd question from Parker here and there while she saw pets in the clinic and drove around the county visiting her large animal patients.

There was a pregnant goat on a farm west of town who wasn't doing so well and Jules spent a lot of time doing ultrasounds and check-ups on the maaa-to-be. Parker sent Jules texts whenever she had questions about the rescue or the house, and she'd taken to sending Jules a few pictures a day of cute things the bunnies did.

On Thursday, Parker brought Buck to the clinic for his neuter appointment and Jules showed her around a bit. She introduced her to Shawn, her veterinary technician, and Nina, her receptionist, and gave her a tour of the small building. It wasn't much, but it was all Jules needed.

"You ready, little guy?" Parker asked when it was time to relinquish the small pet carrier with the scared little Dutch rabbit in it. "It'll be okay – I have it on good authority that Dr. Wakefield is excellent at what she does."

"Sure am," Jules answered. "He's my first patient

today so it won't be long at all before he's recovering comfortably with painkillers."

"And I can come pick him up this evening?" Parker asked. It was cute how concerned she was about this rabbit she hardly knew – it reassured Jules that she'd picked the right person to run the rescue.

"Yep," Jules said. "I'll..." She was about to say *I'll have Nina give you a call,* like she did with every other one of her clients, but this time, she decided to take a personal interest. The more she explained to Parker this time around, the more efficient future visits would be. "I'll call you when he's alert enough to go home, and we'll go over his post-op care together."

She didn't exactly have all afternoon to go over those standard details – again, something Nina was perfectly capable of doing – but Parker relaxed visibly as soon as she'd offered so it was worth the extra time.

"Okay, say goodbye to Parker, little buddy," she said, taking the carrier from her. "I'll take good care of him."

"I know you will," Parker said. "Thank you."

Buck got through his surgery with ease and Parker brought her notebook with her when she came to pick him up. She took copious notes and then gingerly walked with him in his carrier out to her car, ready to spend the evening nursing him out of his anesthesia haze.

The next time Jules saw Parker was the following afternoon. She'd caught up on patient work early and shut down the office so she could head across town to the grocery store. She was just rounding the corner into the cereal aisle when she ran smack into Parker holding a full basket.

"Hi," Jules said. "How's our boy?"

"Much better today," Parker said. "He was really groggy yesterday though."

"To be expected," Jules said. "He's taking his pain meds, eating and eliminating normally?"

"Yep," Parker said. "And I think he's been enjoying his time in the house. I bet he'll be ready to be adopted soon."

"Good," Jules said. Then she noticed the contents of Parker's basket – it was filled with fresh veggies, along with some canned and boxed goods. "Not feeling confident with the vegetable garden yet?"

"It's going well, actually," Parker said. "But I reopened my Etsy shop and got a flood of orders from customers who were waiting on me, so I decided to stock up on ingredients and also celebrate with some comfort food."

Jules reexamined the contents of the basket and noticed refried beans, tortillas, rice, and enchilada sauce. "Mexican night, huh?"

"Yeah, my mom's enchiladas are the best and I miss her," Parker said, and then she did that thing Jules couldn't bear – the thing where people said something alluding to their alive-and-well parents and then their faces got all sad and regretful as they realized who they were talking to. Usually, they couldn't help but comment on it after they realized their error, but instead, Parker said, "Hey, what are you doing for dinner?"

Her eyes flitted to the half-gallon of milk and the frozen lasagna in Jules' hands, and she had to admit, "Nothing that won't keep for another..." She checked the expiration date on the lasagna. "...twelve months."

"Would you like to come over?" Parker asked. "Try my mom's famous enchiladas and let me feed you as a thanks for everything you've done to help me already."

"I don't want to impose—" The idea of going back inside the house, for a whole meal and not just a quick errand, made Jules' chest constrict.

"It's the least I can do," Parker insisted, and then she was giving Jules big, irresistible puppy dog eyes. "Besides, you're the only friend I have in Camden so far and it's Friday night. If I'm not keeping you from any other plans, I'd love to have you over."

The puppy dog eyes were what did it – that and the fact that Jules was sure the invite was genuine – not just extended out of pity. And she really didn't have anything better to do – she'd become a workaholic over the last year and other than her veterinarian friends, who she mostly saw in the context of work, she didn't socialize much. What excuse could she possibly offer?

"Well, I'm not one to turn down a meal," Jules said, watching a smile spread across Parker's face. "What should I bring?"

"Dessert?" Parker asked.

"What do you like?"

"Surprise me." Her eyes dipped down to Jules' mouth as she said it, just for a split second, fast enough that Jules figured she'd imagined it. It was going to be a hell of a long night – a hell of a long twelve weeks, in fact – if she couldn't even share a grocery store aisle with this woman without thinking how beautiful she was.

"You got it," Jules said, clearing her throat and taking a step toward the end of the aisle. "Well, I better get going. What time should I be there?"

"Six," Parker said. "I'm looking forward to it."

Jules nibbled her lip. "Me too," she said, surprised to find that she really was.

When Jules pulled up in front of the farmhouse promptly at six, she let her truck idle there for a minute, still getting used to the surreal feeling of being a guest there. Parker didn't come out to greet her – she was probably in the kitchen at the back of the house and hadn't heard her pull up – and for a moment, Jules was stuck in indecision.

It seemed presumptuous to just let herself into what was now Parker's house, and weirdly formal to ring the bell when she still technically owned the place.

Had her fingers ever touched the doorbell in all her years? Maybe once or twice to play Ding Dong Ditch with her friends when she was a kid. Never actually asking to be let in.

In the end, she was just raising a fist to knock on the frame of the screen door when she saw Parker coming up the hall.

"Hey," she called. "Just come in – you don't have to knock!"

"I didn't want to presume..."

"Nonsense," Parker said, opening the screen door and taking Jules' hand to bring her toward the kitchen. "Come on – dinner's almost done. I hope you're ready to eat like, half a dozen enchiladas."

She pulled her inside so fast Jules didn't even have time to overthink going across the threshold.

"My mouth is watering already," Jules said. "I hope you like cherry pie."

"Who doesn't?" Parker asked, releasing Jules' hand and leading the way back down the hall.

They passed the formal dining room, which her parents used more for conducting interviews with potential rabbit adopters than for meals. When was the last time she'd had a meal in this house? For that matter, when had she last had a genuinely home-cooked meal anywhere? Jules had been so busy with her work and maintaining the rescue that most of her meals lately had come out of either the freezer section or a takeout bag.

"I hope you don't mind eating in the kitchen," Parker said. "It just seemed like the big dining table would be overkill for the two of us."

"Couldn't agree more," Jules said. "My parents and I

always preferred the kitchen table too. The dining room was for holidays and funerals."

God, why had she said that last part?

Parker turned and looked into her eyes, but thankfully, her gaze contained none of the stomach-turning sympathy that Jules usually got from people when funerals came up. She just took the pie and set it on the kitchen counter, saying, "My ex always insisted on eating at the dining table. Even on nights when we didn't have much to say to each other, I don't think we ever ate on the couch."

"I eat all my meals on the couch at my apartment," Jules said. "Did you, uh, break up recently?"

It was nosy and she knew it, but she couldn't help her curiosity. Thankfully, Parker didn't seem too bothered. She said, "Yeah, in May. We were together for twelve years — high school sweethearts, I guess you'd call us — but we just got to a point where we didn't want the same things anymore."

Parker's gaze darkened and Jules could tell there was a bit more to it than that, but she didn't press.

"What about you?" Parker asked. "You haven't mentioned a partner."

Jules smiled. "Nah – I haven't had the time, and it's not like Camden is swimming with options." She studied Parker for a moment longer, then decided to take a chance. She said, "I had a few girlfriends in college and vet school, though."

Recognition flickered in Parker's eyes, then she said, "Just didn't work out?"

Jules shook her head. "I was young and immature. Not ready for anything serious."

"Well," Parker said after a moment, "sit wherever you like. It's your house, after all."

She turned toward the oven to tend to the enchiladas and Jules thought about correcting her – it was Parker's place now, in spirit if not legally. But it'd be easier to get through this meal if she kept things light and didn't think so much about her parents.

So she sat in the chair that had always been her place at the small round table in the corner of the kitchen. It was near the sliding glass door that led to the covered porch, and the back yard beyond it. As a kid, Jules would eat her cereal on school mornings while she watched her mom trudge out to the barn to clean and feed the rabbits, come rain or shine. And she said, "So, tell me more about your treats. What makes them so irresistible to rabbits?"

Parker laughed. "It's just oats, carrots, bananas and hay. I like to mix in other rabbit-friendly foods around the holidays. Pumpkin for the fall, strawberries in the summer, things like that. But what's really starting to get people's attention is this birthday cake I made for my best friend's bunny."

She set the casserole dish in the center of the table and handed Jules a spatula.

"Help yourself!"

"Wait," Jules laughed. "Back up. A bunny birthday cake?"

"Yeah," Parker said, and Jules could tell she was trying to be modest, but the smile on her face gave her away – she was proud of this idea. While Jules wrestled a steaming hot enchilada out of the pan, Parker took out her phone and scrolled through her photos until she found the one she wanted. "Here – that's Ivan on his third birthday."

She held out her phone, where a pure black Flemish giant sniffed curiously at a rabbit-sized two-tier cake made of treats.

"It even has icing!" Jules said, surprised. "That's the cutest damn thing I've ever seen."

"I made it on a lark, but Ivan loved it and as soon as Kani – that's my friend – posted the pictures, people started begging to place orders of their own," Parker said. "I haven't been able to fill many of them yet because of all the moving I've been doing, but now that I'm up and running again, it's full-steam ahead for bunny birthday cakes."

"That's a winner of a product," Jules said. "I mostly focus on large animal medicine, but I treat a few dogs and cats at my office and people are crazy for their pets."

"They really are," Parker said with a smile. "The best part of my job is seeing all the pictures people send me of their bunnies enjoying their treats."

"You know, I have pamphlets in my waiting room advertising the rescue," Jules said. "They always helped my parents get the word out that there were bunnies in the area who needed homes, and they always got a couple of referrals a month out of it."

"I noticed that when I came in with Buck," Parker

said. "I hope you get some cross-referrals back in the other direction from the rescue."

"Oh, I do," Jules said. "I see way more house rabbits than most vets. Anyway, I was just thinking that you should put something up at the clinic to advertise your treats, too."

"Really?" Parker's eyebrows arched with pleasant surprise. "You'd let me do that?"

"Let you?" Jules said. "I'm always telling people that the treats they buy at pet stores are basically like Cheetos and cookies. I'd love to promote a healthier alternative."

Parker smiled and Jules felt a little pride at having made that happen. "Okay," she said. "Thanks. I'll work something up."

Jules took a bite of enchilada and practically melted into her chair. "Oh man, this is a winner too. Wow."

Parker was positively beaming by then. "Thanks. I'll pass the compliments along to my mom." She started to eat too, saying, "So, your turn – tell me more about your practice."

"I see pets – dogs and cats – but there are a lot of farms around here so I also do a lot of deliveries, health exams, things like that," Jules said. She laughed around an overzealous bite of enchilada and added, "When you include spaying and neutering the rabbits, which are classified as exotic pets, my dad always teased that I'm one of the most well-rounded vets in the country."

Parker just smiled. "I bet you are. And you run the office all by yourself?"

Jules nodded. "I've got Shawn and Nina, but I'm the

only vet in Camden. I got lucky and took the practice over from a vet who was retiring just after I graduated. He's been a friend of the family for years."

"It's remarkable that you do all that by yourself, and you're so young," Parker told her. "What are you, in your late twenties?"

Jules shook her head. "Thirty. You?"

"Twenty-eight," Parker said. "Anyway, I'm sure your parents are really proud. Or... were. Sorry."

Jules tried to smile, but didn't quite achieve liftoff. There was an awkward silence and she thought Parker was about to finally ask her how they died. Everybody got around to it eventually, and it was never any fun to explain. *My mom had breast cancer but she and my dad were really swamped with the rescue, so she ignored her symptoms for a while, thinking it was nothing. By the time she got diagnosed, it was too late and the cancer had metastasized to her lymph nodes. She died six months later and my dad died just three days after her – from a broken heart or from a myocardial infarction, that's for those who split hairs to decide.*

Yeah, that story was a mile-a-minute thrill ride all right. Jules reached for the spatula and asked, "Want another one?"

Parker smiled. "Sure. And you better have more, too. I don't think there's any Tupperware."

"Yes there is," Jules said, pointing to a cabinet. "Above the fridge."

Parker gave her an incredulous look. "Who keeps it there?"

"My dad," Jules said with a laugh. "He was a tall guy."

"Did he do most of the cooking?"

"Nah, my mom did," Jules told her. "I just think my dad liked to demonstrate his usefulness – they had this after-dinner routine where my mom would complain that she could never reach the Tupperware. She'd swear she was gonna rearrange the whole kitchen 'one of these days' and then my dad would get up, puff out his chest as if it was the biggest show of chivalry to reach into the cabinet with ease and retrieve whatever it was my mom wanted. Then she'd give him a little love tap on the shoulder and tell him he had to transfer the leftovers while she and I did the dishes."

"Now *that* is sweet," Parker said. "They sound like they really loved each other a lot."

You have no idea, Jules thought. Theirs was the only true love story she'd ever seen, but she couldn't tell Parker that without crying, so she just said, "They loved to razz each other, more like."

"Well, if you get me a Tupperware container later, I'd be happy to wash the dishes," Parker said.

"No deal," Jules said. "My mother would rise from the grave just to smack me upside the head if I let you cook *and* host *and* wash the dishes. I'll do them."

"We'll share the task," Parker said. "You wash, I'll dry."

"I can live with that," Jules said.

As she took another bite – the enchiladas really were incredible – she let out a quiet sigh and realized that was as casually as she'd been able to talk about her parents since they passed. She'd certainly never joked about them to anyone in the past year.

Jules looked across the small table, taking in Parker's soft features, her bare shoulders in a floral halter top, her tongue as it snaked out and licked a little bit of enchilada sauce off her bottom lip. She was a pretty remarkable woman and Jules couldn't think of a single place she'd rather be on a Friday night.

Parker caught her looking a moment later and Jules said, "Save room for dessert."

Parker brewed a pot of decaf coffee while Jules washed the dishes. As they worked, she talked a little more about living in Chicago, and Jules learned that she'd come from a small town originally, the same place in Illinois where her parents still lived.

"I knew there was some country girl in you," Jules said. "You got down in the dirt with the rabbits awfully fast on your first day."

Parker smiled and her eyes twinkled. "Are you saying I look like an indoor girl?"

Jules took the excuse to allow her gaze to drag over Parker's body. She was in the same cut-off shorts she'd worn the other day when they went into town together, and she'd pulled her hair back into a messy bun when they started eating. Now a few tendrils hung loosely around her face and she just couldn't be any prettier.

Jules shrugged, giving Parker a teasing look, and Parker smacked her shoulder, never taking her eyes off of Jules. The whole evening had progressed like that, both of them acting in a way that Jules interpreted as flirty. And if she hadn't known about the male ex, she wouldn't even *need* to interpret anything – she'd know that the way Parker was looking at her was coquettish.

She's straight and you're trying to conduct a business deal with her, she reminded herself as the percolator gurgled out the last of the coffee. Parker turned and grabbed a couple of mugs from a cupboard, just as if she'd always been here, and Jules worked on clearing her head.

She went to another one of the cupboards and brought down two dessert plates, then served up the pie. "Should we go out to the porch to eat this?" she asked. "It's peaceful out back and the fireflies should be getting ready to put on their nightly show."

"That sounds nice," Parker said. She carried the mugs and Jules carried the plates, and they sat down next to each other in her dad's old glider. It was nearly nine o'clock, but the days were still long and it was just getting dark.

A few fireflies lit up in the yard, trying to find each other, and Jules handed Parker her pie. They ate. Jules used her foot to gently swing the glider back and forth. She caught the scent of Parker's perfume every once in a while – something vanilla-y that reminded her of fresh-baked cookies and home. They didn't talk at first, but it didn't feel awkward either. It was comfortable, nice.

Then, when they were both finished eating and Jules

couldn't handle any more hot coffee on a summer night, she set her mug aside and Parker said, "You're so lucky you got to grow up here. This is like a little slice of heaven."

"What was it like where you grew up?"

"Rural, but poorer," Parker said. "And my parents and I lived in town so we didn't have views like this."

"Views?" Jules asked. She looked out at the gathering darkness. It'd be pitch black soon, but for now she could still make out the low-growing soybean fields beyond the barn. That was all there was for miles. "When I was a kid, I hated those fields."

"What?" Parker asked, shocked. "Why?"

"It seemed like a waste to me," Jules explained. "Now, as an adult, I understand that the farmer grows the soybeans so people can eat, and he leased the land from my parents so *they* could eat. But when I was six or seven, all I could see was this land with such great possibility for kickball, tag, snowball fights, whatever, and I wasn't allowed on it."

Parker laughed and Jules turned her head to her.

"What?"

"Look at this amazing property you grew up on," she said. "The bunnies alone would have blown my six-year-old mind, but all you wanted was what you couldn't have?"

Parker's gaze was locked onto Jules'. She could just see the reflection of the kitchen light in her eyes, and everything else on the porch was covered in shadows. But the eyes were all that mattered – Parker saw Jules' world through entirely different eyes, and that idea ran through her like a shiver.

Jules nibbled on her lower lip again. *Did* she want what she couldn't have? Almost always. But when she leaned forward impulsively, Parker didn't pull back. Jules kissed her. The glider stopped moving and Parker sank into the kiss, pressing her mouth back against Jules as a barely audible moan escaped her lips.

6

PARKER

Parker pulled back from Jules as soon as she realized what was happening. Stunned, she said, "I can't."

"Of course," Jules said. "I'm sorry. I should go."

"Don't—" Parker started to object, but Jules was already off the glider.

Kani's words came back to Parker's mind, all that stuff about sober thoughts and drunken actions, and she wondered whether she'd been sending Jules signals she was unaware of. Parker liked her – that was undeniable – and she felt comfortable around her. The past few hours had flown by and she'd found herself smiling and even laughing again for the first time in what felt like forever.

But did she like Jules in that way?

She knew she liked that kiss, once she got over the shock of it.

Jules was gone before she'd had time to process it,

disappearing into the kitchen to deposit her mug and plate in the sink. Parker chased after her and caught her just as she was heading for the front door.

"Wait," she said, catching Jules' wrist.

"I shouldn't have done that," Jules said. "It was inappropriate."

A thousand things were spinning through Parker's head in that moment and she didn't have the time to parse them all, so she just said, "I just got out of a long relationship."

"I know," Jules said. "Don't worry – it won't happen again. Thanks for the meal, Parker. Have a good night."

"Night."

She watched Jules leave and stood in the hall long enough to hear her truck tires crunching away on the gravel. She replayed the kiss – and the night as a whole.

What she'd said was true. She *had* just gotten out of a long relationship, one she by no means felt recovered from. But as she went out to the barn and brought Cotton inside to keep her company for the night, she decided that she really had enjoyed the kiss. It was brief but powerful, the sensation of Jules' lips lingering on her skin, and she'd leaned into it.

Wanted it.

Thud!

Parker's eyes flew open at the sensation of something heavy landing next to her. For a split second, she was in a blind panic, wondering whether she'd have the wherewithal to defend herself if she needed to.

Then long, ticklish whiskers brushed her cheek and a warm, fuzzy bunny nose was sniffing around her face.

"Cotton?" she said, cringing and laughing at the same time as she brushed the phantom sensation of whiskers from her cheek. "How'd you get up here?"

She sat up and wiped the sleep from her eyes. The morning sun was streaming through the window and the door of the indoor pen she'd bought was hanging open.

Cotton had found a way out and jumped into the bed with Parker. She didn't look the least bit guilty about the escape, and in fact, she was looking impatiently at Parker. It didn't take a rabbit expert to know that look – it meant *when is the food coming, human?*

Parker shook her head. "What's your secret, Houdini? How'd you manage to get out?"

She scooped Cotton up and carried her downstairs. Since Buck had recovered, she'd been bringing a different bunny into the house each evening to keep her company and get them used to human interaction. But they all went back outside each morning for breakfast and exercise in the outdoor run with the other rabbits.

On the stairs, Parker kissed the top of Cotton's head and ran her fingers through the extra-soft fur between her pure white ears. She looked so much like her childhood rabbit, Snowball, they could have been sisters.

"You're about ready for your forever home, aren't you?" she cooed.

Jack was too, for that matter, and Parker had posted a

few pictures of them on the Wakefield Rabbit Rescue Facebook page. She'd already had a couple of inquiries from potential adopters, and even though she knew it was best for the rabbits, she was having trouble with the idea of letting them go. Who knew you could fall in love in just one week?

As they passed through the covered porch, Parker glanced at the glider and remembered the kiss all over again. Kani would have a field day when Parker told her what happened – she loved to be right.

Parker returned Cotton to her stall in the barn, then went out to the garden to gather the morning's lettuce.

She couldn't think of a reason to touch base with Jules since their kiss, and Jules was probably too busy to reach out to her.

The following night, Parker was sitting on the living room floor with Bugs and Murphy hopping around her, looking for the treats she'd hidden in various cut-up paper towel tubes scattered across the floor. Murphy was smart, sniffing them out, but Bugs clearly subscribed to the *work smarter, not harder* school of thought – he simply waited for Murphy to find a treat and then stole it from him.

"Be nice and share," Parker was in the middle of chastising them when her phone rang. She picked it up and put it on speakerphone as soon as she saw her mom's name on the screen. "Hi!"

She set the phone on the edge of the coffee table and

continued defending Murphy's right to the treats he'd found.

"Hi, bug," her mom said. "I haven't heard from you in a couple of days and I just wanted to check in. How's everything going?"

"I'm sorry," Parker said. "It's been so busy – I meant to call."

"That's okay," her mom told her. "Catch me up now."

Parker thought of the kiss and her cheeks immediately turned crimson. That was definitely the most eventful and confusing thing that had happened since she'd last spoken to her mom, but it wasn't the kind of thing she'd normally lead a conversation with.

"Well, I've got my treat business back up and running, and Jules offered to help me promote it at her clinic," Parker told her. "I had to take one of the rabbits, Buck, in to have him neutered and he spent two whole days lying next to me on the couch, drugged up and adorably pathetic."

"Aww, poor baby," her mom cooed.

"Jules and I have been getting to know each other some more," Parker went on. "I fed her your enchiladas and she said they were amazing."

"Tell me something I don't know."

"Umm... well, she kissed me." She said it before she had the chance to overthink it. She'd told Kani the morning after it happened, and she'd always had the kind of relationship with her mother where she could tell her anything... but this was uncharted territory.

"Really?" her mom asked.

Parker tried to read her tone, and realized that she was attempting to figure out how she felt about the kiss based on how her mother and Kani had reacted. Kani had, predictably, been all for it, ignoring the fact that in both instances involving women, Parker had been on the receiving end of the kiss. She'd insisted that Parker wasn't nearly as passive as she claimed to be, and Parker wasn't sure what to think anymore.

Ever the mind reader, her mom asked, "How did you feel about that?"

Parker let out a long breath, and then everything she'd been bottling up since the kiss came pouring out of her mouth. "I don't know. I've been thinking about it ever since, and I don't know what to think. David and I started dating so young... I've never been with anyone else."

Her mom let the silence hang between them for a moment or two after Parker had talked herself out, then she softly asked, "Do you like her?"

Parker leaned her back against the sofa and closed her eyes. "I do. She's funny and smart and compassionate, and she doesn't like to show off how deeply she cares about the rabbits but it's obvious that they mean the world to her."

She thought about the name tags, each one painstakingly decorated.

"She's working through a lot because of her parents, and she seems pretty insistent on doing it alone, but she's so strong," Parker said. "I admire her, and my heart beats a little faster whenever she's near me, and I definitely wanted her to kiss me, but..."

"But?" Her mom prompted.

"How am I supposed to know what I want?" Parker asked. "I've never even thought about a life beyond David until a few months ago. And now..."

"Now you're not even sure about your sexuality," her mother filled in. They were words Parker hadn't been brave enough to say out loud yet, and a wave of love and gratitude washed over her at having a mother who was willing to say them for her.

Did Jules have that unconditional support when she came out? She'd barely spoken about her parents so far, but when she did, it was always with a deep and obvious love, so Parker hoped so.

"Yes," Parker said. "Exactly. What would you think if I dated a woman?"

"Well, doodlebug," her mom said, and Parker actually sat forward a bit, hoping her mother was about to solve her problem for her. "You're young. You have lots of time to figure out who you are and who you want to be with. But of course, I will love you exactly the same no matter who you're with – just as long as they treat you well."

Parker sighed. A frustratingly truthful non-answer, just like moms could be counted on to give.

Her frustration must have been audible through the phone, though, because her mom added, "Remember that girl you were friends with in kindergarten, who you used to come home every day and talk about? What she was wearing, what she drew in her notebook that day, whether she let you push her on the swings... what was her name?"

"Erica," Parker said with a smirk. "I haven't thought about her in ages."

"Funny," her mom said coyly. "Neither have I. Wonder what brought her to mind?"

7
JULES

I need you!
—*Parker*

It was Tuesday night and Jules was staring at her phone, trying to dissect the three-word text that Parker had sent her – the first one since the disastrous end to their Friday night dinner. Since then, Jules had more or less been avoiding her, totally unsure of how Parker was feeling about that ill-advised kiss.

She'd just been thinking that if she ignored it long enough, the next time they spoke they could pretend it never happened. And then she got that text and the idea flew out the window. Of course, Parker didn't mean she needed Jules *like that*... she was straight, first and foremost, and even if she wasn't, she certainly didn't seem like the type to go from zero to booty call text.

Surely, she just had a question about the rescue, or

wanted to know the location of the fuse box in the farmhouse, or one of a million other benign possibilities.

The problem was that Jules' mind had gone immediately to less wholesome interpretations of those words. She'd been with other women in her life, had a few girlfriends in college and veterinary school, and she could think of quite a few nights that should have been more memorable than the relatively chaste, quick kiss that she and Parker shared. And yet... she couldn't stop thinking about it.

Maybe it was the forbidden nature of it, the fantasy of turning the straight girl. Maybe it was so powerful because Parker was the first woman she'd kissed – the first woman she'd wanted – since her parents died.

Jules was in the middle of mulling all this over, trying to formulate a response that was both innocent and left the door open just in case, when her veterinary technician, Shawn, coughed from the doorway of her office.

Jules looked up and he had one eyebrow raised at her. "Everything okay in there?"

"Yeah, Shawn, everything's great. You headed out?"

She was distracted, tapping a reply into the phone before she could go any further down that rabbit hole.

What's up?

It was vague and uncreative, but it was the best Jules could do.

"Yeah, I'm leaving," Shawn said. "Don't forget, I'm

taking the morning off tomorrow so I can go to my daughter's kindergarten orientation."

"Mm-hmm," Jules said, still thinking about her phone.

"The Wilsons are going to drop their cat off to be spayed at eight a.m.," Shawn added.

"Yup, got it."

"And there's a hungry mountain lion right behind you licking its chops," Shawn said, getting annoyed. When all Jules did was nod, he shook his head and walked away, calling over his shoulder, "Night, Jules."

"Night, Shawn," she said.

Parker replied a moment later.

Someone abandoned a rabbit. Looks awful. Can I bring to clinic?

"Oh, shit," Jules muttered, her heart sinking. She tapped out a quick reply.

I'm already there – hurt or sick?

She could already guess what happened – some inconsiderate asshole with a rabbit they no longer wanted had gotten wind that there was a rabbit rescue near them and they'd dumped the poor thing on Parker. Probably hadn't even had the decency to ring the doorbell. Jules had seen it before, too many times while she was growing up, but she'd hoped Parker could get through more than a week and a half before she had her first dump-and-run.

Jules pushed away from her desk, taking the phone with her as she headed into the exam room across the hall and pulled some supplies out of the cabinets, trying to prepare for whatever came through the door. Her phone pinged again a minute later.

I don't know.

Jules frowned.

That's okay – drive safe and I'll do what I can to help.

She was outside waiting when Parker's little Geo pulled into the parking lot about ten minutes later. Jules met her at her car door. Parker was wearing nothing but a sports bra and a pair of shorts, and her eyes were wide and wet with concern.

"Its fur is so matted, and it's so skinny," she said. "Please tell me you can help it."

I will.

Jules wanted to say that – to promise it would be okay – but she hadn't even seen the rabbit yet and she'd been a vet long enough to know that sometimes, it was too late for promises like that.

Please don't let it be too late, she thought as she looked into Parker's back seat and saw a cardboard box, open at the top. Inside, there was what looked like a wadded-up length of blue cotton fabric, a few tufts of matted fur poking out here and there.

"I wrapped it in my T-shirt," Parker explained as she opened the back door and picked up the box. "I didn't know what to do."

"You did the right thing," Jules said, taking the box from her. "I need to examine the rabbit. Do you want to come help me?"

Parker nodded, then trailed Jules inside. Shawn was long gone, and so was Nina. The building was empty except for Jules, Parker, and the unfortunate creature bundled up in Parker's T-shirt.

"This way," Jules said, nodding toward the exam room. "Where did you find this little guy?"

"On my front porch," Parker said. "Well, *your* front porch."

Just as Jules had feared, unfortunately. She asked, "Did you see who left it, get a vehicle description or anything like that?"

"No." Parker shook her head. "I was in town dropping off some treat orders at the post office and when I got back, the box was in front of the door."

"Assholes," Jules grumbled. She set the box on the exam table and reached inside, carefully lifting out the little bundle. "Poor baby... let's have a look at you."

She pulled back the layers of T-shirt to reveal a thin brown rabbit with severely matted fur and crust around its ears. Parker was right – it was in bad shape – but Jules was relieved to see it raise its head, looking anxiously around the room. At least the rabbit had enough energy to be scared.

"It's okay," Parker said, instinctively reaching out to calm it. "Dr. Wakefield is going to help you. Right, Jules?"

She looked at Parker, her heart tightening in her chest as she locked onto those pretty eyes. God, she wanted to help... she hoped that she could. She reached for her stethoscope and tucked the ends into her ears, telling Parker, "I'm going to do everything I can. Want to help me do the exam?"

Parker nodded eagerly. "What should I do?"

"I need to listen to its heart and lungs. Keep the rabbit steady on the table," she said. "Talk to it, keep it calm."

It seemed too weak to make any serious attempts at escape, and Jules was used to handling thousand-pound horses on the regular so she'd have no problem doing this solo, but Parker seemed proud to be of use. She crouched down at the head of the table so she could be at eye-level with the rabbit, gently bracing her hands on either side of it and cooing soothing words.

Jules caught an accidental glimpse right down Parker's bra, where the curves of her breasts swelled each time she took a breath, and she averted her eyes.

"This good?" Parker asked.

"Perfect," Jules said without looking at her again. She slid the stethoscope under the rabbit's belly, listening to its breathing and heart rhythm. She looked in its ears and eyes, narrating her actions for Parker's sake. "Heart and lungs sound good. Definitely has a bad case of ear mites, but the eyes look healthy."

"That's not so bad, little buddy," Parker said to the rabbit as Jules continued her exam.

"I don't see any obvious injuries. Let's check the belly."

She palpated along the rabbit's stomach, then with Parker's help, they raised it onto its back feet and Jules checked for signs of distension, urine scalding and other common problems for abused rabbits.

"Looks good – aside from the obvious fur matting and malnourishment," she said as she motioned for Parker to set the rabbit back down. "And it's a boy. A poor, neglected little boy who was very lucky to make your acquaintance when he did, even if his previous owner *is* scum of the earth."

"What do we do now?" Parker asked.

"Start fattening him up," Jules said. She didn't mention the ugly details – that rabbits had a very low tolerance for hunger and empty stomachs, and this one might not have lasted much longer without their intervention. "He'll also need medicine for the ear mites, and until that's cleared up, he can't be around any other rabbits or it'll spread like wildfire."

"For how long?" Parker asked.

"About two weeks to be safe," Jules said. "I'd like to keep him overnight and give him his first few meals via syringe to make sure his digestive tract is moving. And I'll probably have to shave him – once the fur gets matted like this, it's almost impossible to brush out."

Parker stood and Jules averted her eyes again,

focusing on the rabbit instead of the smooth contours of Parker's exposed stomach. "Can I stay?"

"Huh?"

"To help you," she said. "I'd feel horrible dumping a rabbit on you out of the blue and asking you to work late all by yourself."

"It'd be far from the first time – that's the life of a small-town vet. Besides, my apartment is just upstairs."

"Still," Parker said. "I want to help, as long as I'm not just going to get in your way."

Jules smiled. "Stay here. Make sure he doesn't try to jump off the table."

Parker nodded and Jules left the exam room. She went into her office and opened a file cabinet where she had a stack of clean scrub tops and pants for surgery days. She grabbed one of the tops and went back to the exam room, handing it to Parker.

"Here," she said. "It's not that I'm not enjoying the view, but I wouldn't want you to get scratched or bitten."

Parker took the shirt, then looked down at her exposed bra and instantly turned beet red. "Oh my God, I forgot. You know, in the panic of the moment—"

"It's fine," Jules hurried to say. "Don't be embarrassed."

The last thing she wanted was to make her feel bad, or exposed. Parker gave her a bashful look, then pulled the scrub top over her head. They stood there in silence for a moment, Jules nibbling on her lower lip and thinking about that damn kiss again, and then Parker surprised her by saying, "You were enjoying the view?"

Her words sounded coy, but the look she gave Jules was more like that of a middle school girl trying to figure out how to flirt. It made sense, if Parker had only ever been with men before, as Jules was assuming... but then again, she was also assuming that Parker was trying to flirt with her. Maybe her tone had been more accusatory than Jules originally thought.

At a loss for how to answer, Jules just rolled her eyes and said, "You know you're hot. Now let's get back to work. We should take this little guy down the hall and put him on the scale so we have a baseline weight."

"He needs a name," Parker said. "We can't keep calling him 'little guy'."

"Got something in mind?"

Parker nodded. "Lucky."

Jules laughed. "I think we should wait until *after* the shaving and mite treatment is done before we ask him how lucky he feels. *Lucky* would have been going to a good family right away and never getting into this condition in the first place."

"Sometimes lucky is being exactly where you need to be, exactly when you're supposed to be there," Parker said.

She was standing in the doorway, blocking Jules' path, and somehow, she managed to look even more attractive in a loose-fitting scrub top than in nothing but a sports bra. The damn V-neck was practically daring her eyes to follow its hem down into Parker's cleavage. Jules chewed on her lip for a second, wondering what it was about this woman that made the air feel like it had an electric current running through it.

She shook the idea away and said, "Come on, I'll show you how to work the small animal scale."

8

PARKER

*L*ucky seemed aware of just how like his namesake he really was. He sat patiently while Parker and Jules weighed him, hardly squirmed at all when Jules administered the medicine that would clear up his ear mites, and he even tolerated the tedious task of shaving off all his matted fur.

Jules performed the entire job with a stern look of concentration on her face, careful not to nick any of the rabbit's skin with the small electric shears. And while she was focused on Lucky, Parker got the chance to observe Jules.

She was so gentle, yet efficient. She asked Parker to keep Lucky calm, but in reality, she seemed perfectly capable of both soothing and fixing up this poor, small animal all by herself. She wielded the shears expertly, and Parker noticed that she had a tendency to nibble on her lower lip when she was concentrating hard – like when she got to the tricky angle of Lucky's shoulder blade.

Lucky endured the shaving bravely and without a single nick, and by the time Jules was done, he looked less disheveled and seemed to have a bit more energy.

"I think he's feeling better," Parker said as Jules switched off the clippers. "Although he does look a bit like a sheep that's just been sheared."

"That wouldn't be far off if he were an Angora," Jules said. "They're bred for their wool."

"What type of rabbit do you think Lucky is?"

"It's hard to say with the matting and malnutrition," Jules said. "He's big though –maybe a Flemish or American giant."

"Well, whatever he is, I'm going to make sure he's a well-loved house rabbit from now on," Parker said.

Jules smiled at her, and their eyes met. For the first time since she arrived at the clinic, Parker became aware of the fact that they were alone here and she thought of the kiss – and how Jules had abruptly run off afterward. Parker didn't know what to say, or if she should say anything, and so she'd tried to leave Jules alone for a few days.

She was still mulling it over herself – how good it felt, how she felt about it – and trying to process the advice she'd gotten from her mom and Kani.

After she got over her initial shock and amusement, Kani tried to be helpful. They'd talked on Skype the previous night and Kani had asked, "So now that you've had time to think it over, how did it feel?"

"I don't know. It happened really fast and I wasn't expecting it... or maybe I was, subconsciously. It was definitely different from kissing David..."

She trailed off, thinking, and Kani asked, "Better?"

A smile came involuntarily to Parker's lips. "Yeah."

"Then you should try it again," Kani suggested. "When you're ready, of course. Be open to the possibility and see where it takes you. You're never too old to learn something new about yourself."

"Maybe," Parker had said, and then she was shaking her head, feeling frustrated at the bad timing, the confusing emotions flowing through her, the fact that she'd spent a surprising amount of time thinking about Jules since they'd met just a week ago. "You know, this whole situation would be so much less complicated if you hadn't forged that stupid essay!"

"What?" Kani was caught off-guard. "Yeah, if I hadn't done it, you wouldn't be there at all."

"I should just tell her," Parker said. "The longer I'm here with this secret hanging over me, the more I fall in love with the bunnies and... and get tangled up in Jules' life. I need to tell her before she finds out and disqualifies me."

"No," Kani snapped. "Don't be stupid, Parker. She'll never find out on her own and she doesn't need to know – you read the essay yourself. Not a single thing in it was a lie – I just helped you write it."

"You wrote and submitted it."

"Semantics!" Kani insisted. "Parker, do not tell her. It wouldn't be for her sake – it'd only be to assuage your own guilt, and subconsciously you're probably just chafing against the fact that you've actually got something *good* in your life right now after twelve years of shit."

"It wasn't all shit," Parker objected.

"But enough of it was," Kani said. "You deserve this. Jules chose you based on who you are and the work you do. Don't fight it."

Don't fight it. Parker thought about that advice now, and even though she hadn't completely decided to keep her mouth shut about the essay, it was good advice for life in general.

She opened her mouth, about to apologize for her reaction to the kiss, when Jules said, "How's everything going at the rescue? I got busy this weekend and couldn't come by."

"It's going okay," Parker said. "I've been trying not to pester you too much."

Both lies – she could see in Jules' eyes that she was avoiding Parker just as much as Parker had been avoiding her. Did she regret the kiss? Probably, considering how Parker had pushed her away afterward.

"You're not a pest," Jules said, going to a cabinet along the wall and coming back to the exam table with a small bag of something green and powdery, plus a bowl and a thin syringe.

"What's all that?"

"Lucky's dinner," Jules said, and at the mere mention of food, Parker's stomach let out an audible grumble.

"Sorry," she said. "It's not that whatever that is looks particularly appetizing, but I haven't eaten yet."

It was close to eight already, according to the clock on the wall behind Jules, and on an ordinary night, Parker would have eaten at least two hours ago and she'd be sitting on the couch by now, watching one of the rabbits explore the living room.

"Me neither," Jules said.

"That's my fault," Parker apologized. "I showed up with Lucky and threw off your whole evening. I hope you didn't have plans."

"Nah," Jules said. "You weren't interrupting anything more exciting than my evening run, maybe a trip to the gym to use the weight machines if I ended up feeling particularly ambitious."

Parker's eyes went to Jules' upper arms. They weren't visible right now, beneath the bulky sleeves of her scrub top, but Parker had seen quite a bit of them in the tight-fitting tank tops and tees that Jules favored whenever she came out to the rescue. Those muscles spoke of strength and discipline, and Parker wondered what it would feel like to have them wrapped around her.

"I'm sorry I kept you from your workout then," she said.

Jules' eyes met hers for just a second and there was a little spark in them as she said, "I'm not." Then she opened the bag of green powder and said, "Let's give Lucky his dinner, and then if you want to stick around a little longer, we can order something for ourselves. Sound good?"

"Sounds great."

Jules showed Parker how to reconstitute the

powdered Timothy grass with a little bit of water from the sink behind her until it reminded Parker of a green smoothie. Then Jules pulled it into the syringe and Parker held Lucky in place while she fed it to him. He squirmed at first, resisting the foreign object that Jules was poking into his mouth, but as soon as he realized it was his dinner, his jaw started working and his tiny tongue poked out to lap up the liquid.

"Atta boy," Jules said as Lucky took a full syringe, and then another. He turned his head away at a third one, and Jules told Parker to set him down on the floor of the exam room so he could explore his surroundings. "He'll get his energy back soon, once he's got some nutrients in his system. In the meantime, I'll go grab some take-out menus. Be right back."

Parker sat on the floor with Lucky in her lap and waited for him to get curious enough to climb down and start looking around. He was sniffing at the stainless steel legs of the exam table, probably picking up scents from the dogs and cats that had passed through this room before, when Jules came back holding a small stack of menus.

"Pizza, Chinese or Mexican?" she asked.

Parker pursed her lips in thought. "Does a woman who looks like you eat pizza?"

Jules raised an eyebrow. "What's that supposed to mean?"

"I've seen your abs," Parker said. "They're not pizza abs."

Jules smiled coyly, then hooked one finger under the

hem of her scrub top and inched it upward until her belly button was showing, along with a row of subtle but defined abdominal muscles. "Oh, these?"

Parker blushed, and it seemed like all the awkwardness after their kiss had burned off. It was a relief – Parker was beginning to think of Jules as a friend at the very least and she missed the banter that they naturally fell into while they worked around the rescue. "Yeah, those."

She couldn't bring herself to look at Jules when she knew she'd be staring right back at her, but she'd stolen a few glances at her body here and there – those strong arms when Jules hefted a bag of rabbit pellets over her shoulder, her toned abs when she bent over in the garden and her shirt rode up, and the subtle curves of her small breasts when she picked up a rabbit and held it close.

Parker could appreciate the gentle curves of a woman's body, the soft features of a pretty face, in a movie or on the pages of a magazine. Who on earth couldn't acknowledge the soft allure of the fairer sex? But Jules, with her more androgynous blend of the masculine and the feminine, did something entirely new to Parker.

Jules laughed and dropped her shirt hem, then said, "The reason I run is so I can eat all the pizza I want. What do you like on yours?"

"Mushroom, onion and green pepper."

Jules wrinkled her nose at Parker.

"What?" she demanded.

"Mushrooms are gross," Jules said. "I'll order it half and half. My half's gonna be smothered in sausage."

Parker made a gagging gesture, pointing her finger down her throat, and Jules laughed as she walked away to place the order.

Twenty minutes later, they were sitting on the couch in Jules' apartment upstairs, a pizza box on the coffee table in front of them and Lucky cautiously appraising the new space. Parker did much the same, looking around the sparsely decorated apartment. It was practical and functional, just like Jules.

Lucky raised up on his back feet, sniffing at the pizza, then took a nibble out of the corner of the cardboard box. Jules had to catch it before Lucky pulled the whole thing onto the floor.

"Pizza for us, box for the bunny," she said, laughing. She nudged it farther away from the edge of the coffee table, then lifted the lid and they each grabbed a slice. Lucky hopped around the room, exploring, and Parker took it as a good sign – he wouldn't look quite right until his fur grew back, but he was much perkier now.

"What's next for him?" Parker asked after her first bite of delicious, veggie-covered pizza.

"Overnight monitoring," Jules said. "More syringe feedings until he's ready to eat hay and greens on his own again. You can take him home after that, as long as you've got a place to keep him away from the other bunnies. And I'll need to keep monitoring his ears to make sure they heal properly."

"That sounds like a lot," Parker said. "How much will it cost you?"

The orders were trickling into her Etsy shop again

now, and she was still intent on paying Jules for her work, but she knew she didn't have enough yet to cover an emergency medical bill.

Jules must have seen the concern in Parker's eyes, though, because she shrugged it off. "Don't worry about it. I told you the clinic and the rescue have a symbiotic relationship. You just make sure you refer Lucky's adoptive family back to me."

Parker furrowed her brows. "That can't possibly be a fair arrangement."

Jules shrugged again. "It all comes out in the wash."

"Maybe when the rescue was run by your parents," Parker insisted. "You were doing them a favor. But you're giving me their house and their business for the price of an essay. I can't let you do pro bono veterinary care indefinitely too. I want to pay you."

Jules set down her pizza and Parker could see pain etched across her features. It was alarming – in the short amount of time that she'd known Jules, Parker had already learned that she didn't show her true emotions easily. She'd seen a few insincere smiles and heard a few forced laughs, but she'd never actually seen raw emotion. Parker reached out and took her hand. Jules flinched, but didn't pull away.

Her lips were pressed so tightly together that all the color had gone out of them, and it came flooding back when she spoke. "Look, my parents passed pretty unexpectedly. My mom had breast cancer and because she was so busy with the rescue, we didn't even find out until after it had metastasized throughout her body. My dad died three days after she did, and I never really said goodbye to either of them. The rescue is their legacy and I need it to stay open. If donating my time as a vet will help you keep it operational, it's a small price to pay."

Her voice cracked a bit and Parker wondered if Jules had said this out loud to anyone before. She was still obviously struggling through the grieving process, and all Parker could do was squeeze her hand.

"I know the rescue doesn't bring in much money," Jules said. "And you're just getting your treat business back up to speed. Let me worry about the vet bills, okay?"

"Okay," Parker said. It really did feel like an electric current was running through Jules, into Parker's palm and straight into her core.

Jules put her other hand on top of Parker's and they just sat like that for a moment, barely breathing.

"Thank you," she said at last, then released Parker's hand. That forced smile was back as she added, "Better eat up before it gets cold."

She reached for her slice of pizza and Parker did the same. Lucky continued hopping around the room and they watched him in a silence that felt comfortable.

9

JULES

Jules kept Lucky with her in the apartment that night.

It was a quarter to ten by the time she walked Parker back downstairs to her car. She had surgery the next morning – the Wilsons' cat – but the late night was worth it, for Lucky's sake of course but also because all the awkwardness that she'd created with that kiss had melted away. It hadn't even felt terrible to talk about her parents, like it usually did. She and Parker said goodnight and Jules made sure Parker was safely in her car before she headed back up to her apartment.

The next morning, she sent Parker a photo of Lucky with a little green moustache leftover from his breakfast.

He's doing great – pooped overnight so we know his digestive tract is moving.

Parker texted back a few minutes later with a photo

of her own – a selfie in which her long hair was tangled with bedhead... freaking adorable... and she had a big grin and a thumbs-up for Lucky.

> *Way to go, Lucky! This must be how proud parents feel when their kids poop in the potty for the first time.*

Jules brought Lucky downstairs with her and monitored him off and on all day, and by the evening she was confident that he was out of the woods. She called Parker to see if she'd figured out a way to keep him isolated from the other rabbits while his ear mites cleared up, and Parker said she'd make him her sole house bunny for a while.

"You *are* a lucky boy," Jules told him when Parker came to pick him up that evening.

"I've been thinking about it and I want you to know I'm going to find a way to pay you for your work," Parker said. "The spaying and neutering, Lucky's care – all of it. I can't give you money right now, that's true, but maybe I could work off the debt."

"Parker, seriously," Jules said. "It's not a big deal. The ear mite medicine and the powdered hay cost me twenty bucks each, and the rest is just labor. I already told you I didn't have anything going on yesterday—"

"But you're good at your work and you shouldn't do it for free," Parker insisted.

"Thank you," Jules said. "How about this? I'll let you know if I think of anything you can do for me, and otherwise, I'll just open you a tab at the clinic. Pay what you can, when you can."

Parker laughed and held out her hand. "It's a deal."

They shook on it, and she really didn't expect to come up with anything – she had two full-time employees as well as a couple of vets in her network who helped out from time to time – but as it happened, something came up just two weeks later.

Jules had been making almost daily trips out to the McCade farm, where there was a pregnant goat, Mabel, who'd been having a hell of a time. She was getting nearer and nearer to her kidding date and Jules could tell she was going to need to assist the birth.

But on the morning that John McCade called to say that Mabel appeared to be having contractions, it was a Saturday and Jules couldn't secure any of her usual help.

Shawn was coaching soccer practice for his kids and couldn't get away.

Nina was strictly the phone-answering, billing type. Jules had once asked her for help carrying a wounded dog into the exam room and she'd done it, then vomited into the sink when she saw the blood on her hands.

And Marley, the private practice veterinarian from nearby Granville that Jules sometimes called for help, was out of town for a medical conference the whole weekend.

"Shit," Jules muttered. She could birth the kid by herself if she had to, but it was always safer – for herself as well as for Mabel and her baby – to have an extra set of hands.

She momentarily considered John, but small-town life being as familiar as it was, she'd once seen him shear the bolts right off a tire he was trying to change and that sort of brute force could be dangerous for today's task.

She picked up her phone one more time and called Parker. When she answered, Jules said, "Hey, what have you got going on this morning?"

"Just the usual," Parker said. "Rabbits are fed and I'm all caught up on treat orders. I was going to let some of them out for playtime in a little bit. Why?"

"I thought of a way for you to start repaying your vet tab," Jules said. "If you really want to."

"I do."

"Don't agree until I tell you what the job is," Jules said with a chuckle.

Jules already knew from watching her interact with Lucky that Parker would be the perfect person to keep Mabel calm, but she wasn't sure how Parker would handle the gorier details of the kidding process. There were mucous plugs and amniotic fluid just like in a human birth, and it wasn't everyone's cup of tea.

But Parker turned out to have a strong stomach and a gentle touch. She showed up at the address Jules had texted her, the McCade farm west of town, in a pair of overalls and the galoshes that used to belong to Jules' mother.

"I hope you don't mind," Parker said as soon as Jules saw her boots. "I figured this would get messy."

"Hopefully not *that* messy, but I'm glad you're prepared," Jules answered and led her to the barn, where Mabel waited impatiently in a stall and John stood nearby, looking like an anxious father.

"Got yourself a new helper?" he asked when he spotted Parker.

Jules made the introductions, then handed Parker a pair of gloves. "You ready?"

"As I'll ever be," she said, stepping into the stall with Jules.

Parker was the perfect helper. She did everything Jules asked without question or hesitation. She kept Mabel as calm as possible and even managed John when he got antsy and wanted to step into the stall – and get in everyone's way.

After about an hour of contractions without much progress, suddenly a little white hoof appeared.

"Mabel, you're about to be a mama!" Parker said when she saw it.

"The kid's out of position," Jules said. "I need to step in."

It was as she'd expected – this was Mabel's first kidding and it wouldn't be simple. Jules had to manually adjust the position of the kid, and while she was doing it, she felt a second set of hooves.

"Well, John, looks like you're getting two new babies on the farm today," she said. "And I think they're fighting over who gets to be the firstborn."

The kids were in a hurry, both moving toward the birth canal at the same time, but even still, it took another two hours before both had been birthed, dried off and examined. Mabel managed the whole thing gracefully, and by the end, she lay in clean, fresh hay with her two beautiful kids curled up against her.

Jules stripped off her gloves and told Parker she could do the same, and they both stepped out of the stall, exhausted and filthy but satisfied with a successful birth.

"We're done?" Parker asked, using the back of her forearm to wipe sweat from her brow.

"Yep," Jules said. "Two more does added to the herd."

"What do you do with them, Mr. McCade?" Parker asked.

"You ever had goat cheese?" he asked. When she shook her head, he grinned and said, "Come on up to the house, both of ya – you can get cleaned up and then I'm gonna rock your world."

He headed for the house and Jules and Parker followed. While they walked, Parker whispered, "Do you really have an appetite after all that?"

She made a disgusted face with her tongue out and Jules couldn't help but laugh. She said, "After everything I've seen at work, it takes a lot to turn me off my food. You did really well back there by the way – thanks for your help."

Parker smiled. "Did you think I'd faint?"

"Maybe." Jules shrugged. "I didn't know what to expect but I was kind of in a bind, so I appreciate it. Consider Lucky's bills paid off."

"It was actually kind of fun," Parker said. "Gross, definitely, but worth it once the kids were all cleaned up and snuggling with their mama."

John held the kitchen door open for them and they came inside, Jules going down the hall to the bathroom while Parker cleaned up in the kitchen sink. By the time Jules returned, John had a pretty impressive cheese plate made up with crackers and sliced figs, as well as three beer bottles looped into his fingers.

"Should we go out on the patio?" he asked.

"Your house, your choice, John," Jules told him, and he led the way to the brick patio on the side of the house. The three of them sat at a table beneath a sun umbrella and he passed around the beers, then talked up his cheese while they ate.

"This particular cheesemaking process has been in my family for four generations," he explained. "We've been goat farmers all the way back to when my ancestors settled this land, although we've branched out just a little bit since then."

He gave a wink and Jules explained to Parker, "You can get McCade goat cheese in grocery stores and farmer's markets all across the Midwest. And how many varieties do you have now, John, seven?"

"Eight," he said proudly. "Just added a pesto goat cheese spread to our offerings last spring."

Parker seemed to get back some of her appetite. She took a cracker and spread it generously with cheese, took a bite, and then smiled approvingly. "Wow, that's incredible. Your family really knows what they're doing."

"Thank you, ma'am," John said, taking a long pull on his beer bottle. "Although it's just me now. Been too busy to have a family so I'm not sure who's going to take over after I get too old. I guess I could always run a contest."

He smirked at Jules, who rolled her eyes and said, "John, you're three years older than me. We went to high school together. You've got plenty of time."

"Yeah, if I can ever figure out where to meet somebody," he said.

"Farmers Only?" Jules suggested.

He snorted and took another drink of beer, damn near emptying the bottle. "I don't think I'm ready to join any dating websites just yet." He took one final pull on his beer, then stood. "All right, I've taken enough abuse from you. Let me get my checkbook so you can be on your way once you're done eating."

He disappeared inside the house, and when it was just Parker and Jules on the patio, she said, "Be honest – what do you think of the cheese?"

"It's a little... pungent," Parker said, taking a more modest nibble from her loaded cracker. "I like it – I just don't think I have very many recipes that would match this flavor."

"That's very diplomatic of you," Jules said, smirking. "John does a good business but goat cheese is not for everyone. Me, for instance."

Parker laughed and took another cracker, adding a little fig on top of the cheese this time. Jules couldn't tell if she genuinely liked it or if she was just being polite. While she ate, Jules sipped her beer and then Parker said,

"It is sad how his family business might end with him if he doesn't come up with something. You were really creative with that contest."

"Well, you know what they say – necessity is the mother of invention," Jules said. "John has a few more good years before he really needs to start thinking about lines of succession. I just wish I'd had the time to talk it over with my parents, make sure they were okay with what I came up with."

"You're doing the best you can," Parker said, taking her hand. "I'm sure they would appreciate that."

The first time she'd taken Jules' hand like that – on the couch at her apartment – Jules had flinched and wanted to pull her hand away. This time, she accepted the comfort, turning her hand over and tangling her fingers in Parker's.

Jules looked toward the house, but there was no sign of John. He was a bachelor through and through, and not the best housekeeper. He was probably tearing the place apart, looking for his checkbook.

Jules looked into Parker's eyes and suddenly, there was a question she had to ask. "Do you think it's possible to die of a broken heart?"

She'd been turning that question over in her own mind for the last year, ever since her dad passed out of the blue so quickly after her mom. She needed someone to tell her she wasn't being ridiculous.

"Are you thinking about your dad?" Parker asked.

Jules nodded.

"I do," Parker said without missing a beat. "I believe

in love at first sight and soul mates and all that mushy romantic stuff because sometimes love hurts us so badly that when we lose someone, it feels like losing our own heart. That kind of pain wouldn't be worth it if all the good stuff wasn't there to balance it out."

Emotion swelled in Jules' chest, and it even started to mist over her eyes. She wanted to kiss Parker again, pull her into her arms and let all that emotion come pouring out.

Instead, John burst through the door, triumphantly waving his checkbook in the air. "Found it! How much d'ya say it was?"

Jules squeezed Parker's hand, then let go and mouthed *Thank you.*

10

PARKER

Parker walked away from the McCade farm tired, more than a little bit dirty from the birthing stall, and feeling better than she had in years.

Watching two new lives coming into the world – at the skilled hands of Jules, no less – was simply magical. Parker couldn't help feeling uplifted, and things felt a little bit easier between her and Jules, too.

"How's our lucky little bunny doing?" Jules asked as they walked toward their cars.

"Good," Parker said. "Although I have to confess, I found it too difficult to send him out to the barn with the others after his ear mites cleared up. He's still in the house."

Jules laughed. "Sounds like you have a pet."

"He got really used to being in the house with me," Parker said, feeling like she had to defend herself. "He even jumps up and sleeps in the bed with me sometimes.

How could I tell him he had to go out to the barn and wait for a fur-ever family?"

"Well, that sounds like the cutest thing that ever was," Jules said. She wasn't the sappy, warm and fuzzy type, but in that moment, there was something soft and longing in her eyes that made Parker's stomach quiver.

She thought about the kiss, about what it might feel like to reach for Jules, to do it again. There were a lot of cracks in her heart that she'd had no idea were even there when she was with David, but somehow, Parker knew that Jules could fill every one of them.

But John McCade was sitting on his patio behind them, drinking another beer, and Parker was covered in goat fluids. This was hardly the right moment to explore that.

"It is," she said to lighten the atmosphere, "until Lucky gets a spurt of energy and does a zoomie over my head at three in the morning."

Jules laughed. "Nope, that sounds adorable too."

They reached their cars and Parker put her hand on the door of her Geo, then Jules said, "Hey, I have an idea."

"Yeah?"

"You've been here a month already, and yet I bet you haven't seen much of Camden," she went on. "Let me show you around. We'll grab a bite to eat at my favorite café and then I'll take you on a walking tour. You can meet some more of the locals."

Parker's heart swelled at the idea – it meant Jules was

getting invested in keeping her around, and Parker was certainly falling in love with this place, the rabbits, the rescue... and she didn't mind spending time with Jules, either. "When?"

"Any night that you're free."

"How about tomorrow?" Parker asked.

"Tomorrow's perfect," Jules said. "I'll pick you up at six."

"It's a date," Parker said, then turned away before an embarrassed smile broke across her lips.

She didn't really mean it – *it's a date* was just one of those automatic phrases people used – but Jules had just agreed to take her out to dinner on a Friday night and every time Parker was around her, the air felt charged, like it did moments before a lightning strike. Parker had no clue what she was doing, what she wanted, how she really felt, but something hopeful was building in her chest as she wondered if it really was a date.

She got in her car and gave Jules a quick wave, then drove away before she could be caught grinning like a damn fool. What on earth was happening to her?

The next night, Parker put on a wrap-around sundress and took the time to carefully flatten her hair so it was long and silky. Most of the time when Jules saw her, Parker had just spent the day down in the dirt with a couple dozen rabbits, and she was definitely wild and unkempt with panic the day she brought Lucky to the clinic.

Whether this was a date or just a friendly gesture, Parker wanted Jules to know she could clean up nicely. But Jules had mentioned a walk, so she made the look a little more casual with a pair of slip-on Converse.

Parker sat on a rocking chair on the front porch after she was ready, trying not to let her imagination run away from her. *Is this a date? Am I overdressed? Should I have gotten advice from Kani?*

She'd intentionally avoided the subject with her best friend because she didn't want to build the night into more than it was, and she knew the minute Kani got wind of it, she'd start asking Parker a million questions about how she felt about Jules, what she wanted to happen and how she expected the night to end.

Parker didn't have answers to any of that, but she was relieved to see that at least she wasn't overdressed when Jules showed up a few minutes before six and climbed out of her truck in a pair of navy Bermuda shorts and a crisp button-up shirt.

"Hey," she said, tilting her chin down and running her fingers through her hair. "You look beautiful."

Parker smiled and looked self-consciously down at herself. "Thanks. I wasn't sure how to dress because you didn't mention the name of the café we're going to eat at."

"It's called Norie's Place," Jules said. "My friend Hannah and her wife, Avery, run it together. It's pretty casual – you'll fit right in."

She held out her hand to help Parker down the stairs – a chivalrous gesture that was completely unnecessary considering her sneakers, but Parker took Jules' hand anyway. It was warm and her skin was soft, and as she walked beside Jules, she inhaled her scent – something rugged and outdoorsy, like pine, that perfectly suited her.

"Are there, umm..." Parker had started to ask whether there were a lot of LGBT+ people in a town as small as Camden. There certainly hadn't been many in Mount Vernon when Parker was a kid – at least not many who were out. But her tongue tripped over the words and she thought better of starting their date-or-maybe-not-date on such a serious subject.

"Yes?"

"Uh, how did you meet Hannah and Avery?" she settled on instead as Jules opened the passenger door for her and Parker hoisted herself into the truck.

"Same way you meet most people in a small town," Jules said. "Bump into them enough times and eventually you start thinking of them as your friends. Plus I went to high school with Hannah's cousins, but we ran in different circles."

Parker laughed. "How many circles were there at Camden High? My own graduating class was about fifty and sometimes I think if there was more than one social group, I wouldn't have ended up with David at all."

"Everything happens for a reason, though," Jules said. "If you didn't date him, you might not be here now."

Parker laughed. "That's true. And if I hadn't gotten

fed up with him chasing his dreams and making me wait on mine, I *definitely* wouldn't be here."

"Well, thank God you did," Jules said.

Parker thought of the essay that got her to Camden. Kani would have never thought to forge it for her if Parker hadn't reached her breaking point with David. And for that matter, Parker may never have met Kani at all if she hadn't been looking for some thin connection to the life she really wanted. It really was a long line of cause and effect leading to this moment.

Tell her. While Jules jogged around to the driver's seat, Parker's conscience reared its head again. She'd been here a month – she was one third of the way through the trial period and getting closer to Jules every day, and yet Jules still didn't know that what had gotten Parker here was a lie.

How much worse would it be if Jules didn't find out until the end of the trial period, when she could have used all that time to train someone else if she wanted to? Or worse yet, after she'd signed her parents' property over to Parker?

She couldn't let that happen. She wouldn't.

Parker opened her mouth, determined to tell the truth as soon as Jules slid behind the wheel, but then Jules surprised her by taking both her hands in Parker's and looking her straight in the eyes. It was such an abrupt, intimate gesture that it stole the words right out of Parker's mouth.

"I just wanted to say something before we head out," Jules told her. "I know your last relationship was a long one and you might not be ready to start seriously dating again, and I also know that you're used to dating men. But I've really enjoyed getting to know you these past few weeks and I like you a lot, Parker. So I wanted to remove any ambiguity there might be and say that I'd love it if tonight could be our first date, but of course I'll take things slow and we'll go at whatever pace you'd like." She glanced down at her lap, her hair falling momentarily into her eyes before she looked back up with a little flick of her head and added, "And if I'm completely misreading the vibe between us, just tell me and we'll go out as friends tonight and I'll never mention it again."

Parker's heart was pounding in her chest. At least that was one less question floating through her mind – Jules *did* want this to be a date.

"You're not misreading anything," she said. "And thank you for saying all that. To be honest, I feel sort of confused and like I shouldn't be ready to move on already, but I'm also pretty sure that's just David's voice stuck in my head, telling me I should keep waiting around for him forever and never take control of my own life."

"That voice is definitely a liar," Jules said. "But I know what you mean. I haven't dated since my parents died because it feels like I should still be grieving."

"I never met your parents but from what I've learned about them, I'm sure they would want you to be happy," Parker said. "And I'd really like it if tonight was our first date."

Jules grinned and released one of Parker's hands so

she could reach into the narrow second row of seats in the pickup. She came back with a bouquet of wildflowers and handed them to Parker. "I was hoping you'd say that."

During the short drive to Norie's Place, Jules held Parker's hand on the bench seat. It was nice – ten minutes to just be together and enjoy that small gesture of intimacy without having to wonder what it meant for the two of them, or for her own sexual orientation.

Bisexual… pansexual… straight with one exception… Parker had never questioned her identity before because she'd always just been with David, and she'd assumed it was forever. Now, Jules was bringing out a whole new side of her and she wasn't sure whether the labels felt like her own or not.

She just knew, in that moment, it felt good to be sitting beside Jules, to have their fingers entwined, to feel the breeze from the open window on her cheeks and the potential of the evening stretching out in front of her.

When it seemed like the silence was getting too heavy, Parker said, "So, my parents keep bugging me about coming out here to see the rescue."

It just popped into her head – the first thing that came to mind because she'd just been on the phone with her mother a few hours ago, nervously chattering about the date. But the moment it came out of her mouth now, she looked at Jules and bit her tongue.

"Sorry," she said. Inside, it was more like, *Way to go. The first thing you do on your date is complain about having parents who want to see you?*

Jules just shook her head. "Don't do that."

"What?"

"Tiptoe around me," she said, squeezing Parker's hand. "My parents are dead. It sucks – a *lot* – but a month ago, I wasn't even willing to say it out loud. I'm not over it and I'm not sure I ever will be, but I'm working on it. Just like you're working on getting over your ex."

Parker instinctively checked for the sensation of that pesky little lump in her throat – the one that never failed to make an appearance when it came to David. But there was nothing. Was there anything left to get over?

"We're a pair," she said, and Jules laughed.

"We are," she answered. "This is either going to end in total disaster or happily ever after."

"Well, I try to be an optimist," Parker told her as Jules pulled up to a parking spot on the curb outside a cute little café with a handcrafted sign that read *Norie's Place*.

"We're here," Jules said. "And hey – you should absolutely invite your parents to come out and visit you. The farmhouse is yours – I don't want you to feel like you're just a visitor there."

"Thank you," Parker said. "I appreciate it."

They went inside and Jules introduced Parker to the owner, Hannah, who did pretty much everything from waiting tables to cooking the food and taking payment, depending on where her staff needed her.

"Avery here?" Jules asked, but Hannah shook her head.

"She's got a big contract with a real estate developer and her crew's been framing houses on the other side of town all week."

Jules narrowed her eyes. "She's not working for what's-his-name, Jason Mansfield, is she?"

Hannah nodded. "It's Justin Manning."

"Yeah, that's right," Jules said with a snap of her fingers, then turned to Parker to explain, "He was hounding me to buy my parents' property last year but he was gonna use the land to build a housing development."

"Aww, and evict the rabbits?" Parker asked with a frown.

"Yeah, but don't worry – I told him to take a hike," Jules said. Then she turned back to Hannah and made introductions. "Parker here is running the rescue now and she's doing a great job of it."

"Ah, so you're the lucky contest winner," Hannah said. "I'll have to tell Avery that we met – we've been wondering who was going to get the golden ticket, so to speak. Anyway, you two grab a table and I'll be right over to take your orders."

She disappeared into the kitchen and Jules pointed Parker over to a cozy-looking table near a big stone fireplace. It was far too hot of an August night for there to be an actual fire, but Hannah had a stack of faux logs set up there with a surprisingly realistic electric fire flickering inside.

Parker sat down and looked around. The café was

relatively crowded, with lots of comfortable seating and rustic country decor. "This place is really neat."

"Avery's a woodworker as well as a contractor," Jules explained. "She made a lot of the tables and chairs here, and some of the wall decor, too, I think. She takes shifts at the café now and then, but she's got her own construction company and she's been doing really well for herself ever since Camden started to develop."

"And I take it you're not a big fan of her employer?"

"Jason-Justin-whatever?" Jules said, wrinkling her nose. "The guy left a bad taste in my mouth – he doesn't care about this town, just wants to cash in. But I'm glad he's hiring local contractors to do the labor – puts money in my friends' pockets."

Hannah came back a minute later – barely enough time for Parker to look over the impressive menu – and took their orders. She brought over a couple glasses of house white, proudly explaining that Norie's Place had just gotten its liquor license, and Parker caught her giving Jules a wink before she headed over to one of the other tables.

"What was that?" Parker asked, unable to suppress a grin.

Jules blushed – actually blushed! – and Parker had to cajole a confession out of her. At last, she said, "She's one half of the most blissfully happily married couple ever and she's been waiting ages for me to find a girlfriend so we could all go out on double dates. But that's just Hannah being Hannah – please ignore her."

"That's sweet though," Parker said. "I want that

someday – the blissful happiness and the couple friends, all of it."

"I do too," Jules admitted.

"How did they meet?" Parker asked.

"Hannah inherited a house from a relative and moved here from New York City," Jules told her. "She had no clue what she was doing in the country and Avery just happened to be her closest neighbor. One night she woke up to a soaking wet Hannah pounding on her door, panicking about a busted water pipe. Avery came to the rescue and the rest is history."

"Aww. Sounds like fate intervened on that one," Parker said just as Hannah arrived with their food – savory crepes that were the seasonal special.

"Are you telling her my stories?" Hannah asked.

"Just one," Jules said defensively. "She asked how you and Avery met."

"Well, the four of us will have to get together sometime and you can tell me how *this* happened," Hannah shot back, waving her finger back and forth between Jules and Parker as if *this* was something significant already.

Jules just rolled her eyes, but Parker surprised herself by agreeing to it, adding, "I'd love to make some new friends in town."

"Set a date," Hannah said, "and I'll let Avery know."

Then she was gone, helping some other customers, and Jules gave Parker a wry look. "Told you she wanted to double date. Let me know if you want to get out of it – I can make up an excuse."

"I don't," Parker said, sliding her foot along the floor

beneath the table until she found Jules' own sneakered foot.

Was all of this – the contest, the rescue, the gorgeous woman in front of her – moving so fast it made her dizzy? Hell yes, but she was loving every disorienting minute of it.

11
JULES

By the time the meal was over, Jules actually felt lighter.

She'd said things to Parker about the grieving process for her parents that she'd never spoken aloud before, and even though it was scary – and totally not first date material – she found she *wanted* to share it. And Parker elegantly sidestepped the awkward, uncomfortable elements of the conversation, never once making Jules feel pitied or lonely.

Instead, they wound up playing footsie beneath the table through most of the meal. Parker nudged Jules first, then withdrew her foot. A minute or two later, Jules returned the gesture, and back and forth they went, unable to stop the game for more than a few minutes at a time. It was a little bit silly, but the levity made what Jules had shared so much easier.

And when they left the café – with a couple of slices

of cheesecake that Hannah had insisted they take *for later* – Parker didn't hesitate to slide her hand into Jules'.

"Where to now?" she asked.

"I *was* going to take you to my favorite ice cream stand," Jules said. "But now we have this cheesecake for dessert."

"Damn that Hannah," Parker teased. "I guess that just means there'll have to be a second date so you can take me for ice cream."

It was getting dark out by then, but Jules could still make out the warmth of Parker's eyes in the waning light. She pulled her to a stop on the sidewalk and turned Parker to face her.

When she'd picked her up at the house, Jules had decided that, rather than continuing to guess and fantasize and possibly overstep her bounds, she was just going to lay everything on the line and tell Parker how she felt. She was fully bracing herself for rejection, for Parker to decide that she wasn't into women after all, or that she wasn't into Jules in particular.

But all through the meal, Parker just kept leaning in, getting closer, opening up. Jules sensed no hesitation and she'd never connected with anyone the way she was connecting with Parker now. It felt good and she didn't want to hold back.

"We're only halfway through our first date and you already want a second one? You sure about that?"

Parker was taller than Jules by at least two or three inches and she looked down into her eyes. It was sexy as hell and the phrase *I wanna climb you like a tree* popped into Jules' head.

Parker only got about halfway through a nod before Jules caught her around the back of the neck and dragged her mouth down to kiss her. Jules inhaled her scent – vanilla, home – and claimed Parker's mouth with her own.

She wanted so much more – she wanted to wrap Parker in her arms and pull her body close so there was no more space between them – but they were standing on the sidewalk with cars going by periodically and pedestrians in the distance.

Jules reluctantly let her go, catching her breath. She nibbled her lower lip and said, "We better start our tour before we get ourselves into trouble."

Jules led Parker on a walking tour of Camden for about an hour. She pointed out the ice cream shop and the library, the future site of the already infamous Amazon Fulfillment Center, and the park with all the trails where she liked to go running. She pointed out at least a dozen other landmarks in the town where she'd spent most of her life, but it was Parker she was most interested in.

They talked – about the differences between big city living and small-town life, about Parker's best friend in Finland and Jules' vet friends in nearby Granville, about their favorite books, movies, musical genres, about Parker's parents and how similar they sounded to Jules' folks.

And when both of them were tired and they'd circled their way back to Norie's Place, they lingered on the sidewalk, neither of them wanting to make the wrong move that would lead to the end of the date.

At last, Parker motioned to the plastic bag that hung around Jules' wrist and said, "Do you think those cheesecake slices are still good? It's hot out tonight."

"Yeah," Jules said, "Hannah included ice packs because she knew we were going to be walking for a little while."

"She really does run a full-service café," Parker said, impressed.

"Just for her friends," Jules said, then smiled and added, "but pretty much everyone who goes to Norie's Place ends up being her friend. So, what do you say? Should we have dessert?"

"I'd love that," Parker said.

"Your place or mine?"

"Do you mind if we go back to my place?" Parker asked. "I need to give the bunnies their evening meal, and Lucky's probably wondering if I'm ever coming back."

"Sure," Jules said, opening Parker's door for her. "I'd love to see our little guy anyway, make sure his ears are still healing up well."

"He looks like a totally different rabbit," Parker told her. "His fur is growing back."

They drove back to the farmhouse and Jules went inside to put the cheesecake slices on plates and check out Lucky's ears while Parker made a pitstop in the barn to tend to the other rabbits.

It was a little strange helping herself to the kitchen once again – she'd just started to think of the house as Parker's instead of her parents' and there she was, making herself at home again. There were little changes, though – small touches that established the space as Parker's.

She'd brought the Tupperware down from the unreachable cabinet above the refrigerator, and she'd hung a corkboard on one wall and turned it into a command center of sorts, mapping out treat orders and adoption appointments with precision.

And there was a new addition in the living room. Jules was just checking it out when Parker appeared in the doorway.

"What do you think? I got it at a yard sale for ten bucks," she said while Jules took in the strange sight of a television in the house.

"My parents hated TV," she said. "They thought it was the twenty-first century opium of the people and whenever I'd whine to them as a kid about some show that all my friends were watching, they'd just tell me to go outside and use my imagination. As an only child, that got old pretty quick."

"So you don't watch much TV then," Parker said.

"On the contrary," Jules answered with a snort. "You should see how much crap I've got in my Netflix queue. On second thought, maybe I should keep the trash TV that I watch to myself. Don't want you to stop respecting me."

"Mm, Fuller House, huh?" Parker teased.

"Hey, I can't just turn off my childhood Candace Cameron crush like that, can I?" Jules asked, snapping her fingers. She handed Parker one of the cheesecake slices on a plate and asked, "Who was your celebrity crush growing up?"

"Don't laugh," Parker said and Jules crossed her heart. "Ryan Phillippe."

"Ah, so you like the pretty boys," Jules said. "Did you ever have a crush on any female actresses?"

"Not that I identified that way at the time," Parker said, putting her finger to her chin and thinking for a minute. "Although I did watch Anna Chlumsky's movies *far* more often than was reasonable. I watched *Gold Diggers* so many times I wore out the VHS."

"Hmm..." Jules considered for a moment. "I feel like a type is emerging. Fair hair, light eyes, pouty lips." She looked down at herself – light hair, blue eyes – and gave Parker a smirk. "I'm one lucky woman."

Parker laughed and said, "I honestly have no idea what my type is when it comes to women, or if I even *have* a type." She took a step closer and added, "I just know I like you."

"And vaguely sapphic teenage love stories," Jules added, and Parker furrowed her brows.

"Huh?"

"*Gold Diggers,*" Jules said. "It's totally a romance in disguise."

"Anna and Christina Ricci are best friends," Parker said, and now it was Jules' turn to arch an eyebrow.

"Wanna bet?"

Parker laughed. "What do you have in mind?"

Jules glanced at the time on her phone. It was only nine o'clock and she didn't mind making up an excuse to extend the date a bit longer, so she said, "If you're not too tired, I bet we can find the movie on Netflix and I'll show you while we eat our dessert."

Parker smiled broadly. "I haven't seen that movie in ages. Honestly, I forgot all about it until just now so I'd love to."

Parker let Lucky out of his pen and gave him free rein over the living room, then plopped down beside Jules on the couch. She pulled up her Netflix account then handed the remote to Jules, who found the movie. As they settled in with their cheesecake, Jules put her arm across the back of the sofa. Parker inched a little closer to her, and by the time they got through the opening credits, they were snuggled up together.

Jules figured Parker would put up a little more of a fight over Jules' assertion that her favorite childhood movie had sapphic romantic undertones, but they got no further than the first scene, in which Christina Ricci's character spies Anna Chlumsky's fighting off a pack of bullies in dreamy slow motion.

Parker laughed and said, "Okay, you win. This movie is totally gay. I can't believe I never saw it before."

"You just weren't looking," Jules said.

Parker snuggled a little closer against her after they both finished eating dessert, and Lucky hopped up on the couch and sniffed at Jules, eventually ending up in her lap while Parker rested her head on Jules' shoulder.

By the midpoint in the movie, both Parker and Lucky were sleeping and in her unconscious state, Parker's head had slid down Jules' chest to rest just above her breast. With every exhale, warm air heated the fabric of her shirt and Jules felt her nipple harden and her core awaken. She wasn't about to wake Parker up, though, and risk bringing all of this to an end.

It had been a perfect first date, in her book, and she wanted it to last as long as possible so she sat still, not disturbing either of them and trying to concentrate on the movie instead of Parker's hot breath against her skin.

Jules opened her eyes at the movement of the screensaver on Parker's television. It was the only light source in the room and she squinted at it for a moment, realizing she'd fallen asleep too.

Lucky had hopped down from her lap at some point and was now stretched out on the rug, having little bunny dreams, but Parker still slept on her chest. Jules ran one hand over the long strands that had fallen over Parker's face, and Parker let out a little groan and lifted her head.

"I'm sorry," Jules whispered. "I didn't mean to wake you."

"What time is it?" Parker asked, her face close to Jules' and their bodies still pressed against each other.

"I don't know," Jules said. Parker's eyes glimmered in the light from the TV, and when she licked her lips, Jules followed the path of her tongue, suddenly feeling hungry.

It was Parker that made the first move, though. She inched closer, her full breasts pressing against Jules' side, and planted her lips on Jules' mouth.

Jules let out a little groan, her body fully awakening to Parker's touch. She deepened the kiss, opening her mouth and circling Parker's tongue with her own as she took Parker's hips in her hands. It was almost as if she'd never woken at all, because this was exactly how she'd fantasized the date would end – although she never really expected it.

Parker was running her hand through Jules' hair, her fingertips traveling down the side of her face and tracing a line over her jaw, then down her neck. She abandoned herself to the kiss and put up no resistance when Jules grabbed her around the waist and pulled Parker into her lap.

"Is this okay?" she whispered, her mouth still pressed to Parker's.

Parker nodded. "I want you."

Jules' pulse was pounding. *You do?* Part of her wanted to analyze what that meant, ask Parker for clarification, figure out her boundaries. But the rest of her desperately didn't want to break the spell they were under so she just let Parker lead the way.

To Jules' surprise and delight, Parker straddled her lap, her thighs pressed firm around her. Jules encircled her waist with her arms and Parker pulled back for a second. Had she overstepped? But Parker just grinned at her, hunger in her eyes, as she ran her hands up Jules' biceps and then wrapped her arms around Jules' neck. Their bodies came together, Parker's core pressed to Jules' lower stomach and their breasts touching.

Jules inhaled a ragged breath as Parker started to rock her hips against her, letting out little moans as she ground herself against Jules and the feel of her breasts, heavy and full against Jules' chest, hardened her nipples.

"God, you're perfect," Jules breathed, feeling herself getting wet as this beautiful woman moved and thrust her hips against her.

She slipped her hands beneath the hem of Parker's dress, which had already crept up to the tops of her thighs. Her fingertips touched soft lace and then cotton, finding the supple curves of Parker's ass beneath her panties, and it was all she could do to keep from taking handfuls of her and squeezing, possessing, consuming.

Jules wanted her so badly her whole body was throbbing, and the desire only amplified when Parker let out a dreamy little moan, pressing her core wantonly against Jules' stomach.

"I've never felt this way before," Parker said, pulling back so she could look at Jules in the low light.

"About a woman?"

"About anyone," she said. "You make me feel like I've been sleepwalking my way through life and now I'm finally awake."

"I want you so bad," Jules groaned, dragging Parker back to her. They kissed again, messy and desperate and passionate, and then Jules broke away one more time. "Tell me where to stop, okay? You call the shots."

"I don't want you to stop," Parker breathed.

Her hands found the buttons of Jules' shirt, expertly working their way down until she had the whole thing undone and her shirt yanked up out of her shorts. Beneath, she was wearing a cotton tank top and nothing else, and when Parker pressed her palms to the thin fabric, finding Jules' pert nipples beneath, it sent an irrepressible surge of desire through her.

She leaned down, kissing Jules softly, and whispered, "Put your hands on me."

"Mmm..." Jules let out a hungry growl and grabbed Parker by the hips, twisting and flipping her onto her back on the couch. Jules landed on top of her, her hips between Parker's legs and her hands sliding up her thighs.

The hem of Parker's dress fell around her waist and Jules got a glimpse of that lace she'd felt with her fingertips, delicate and feminine in the darkness. She could also see a circle of dampened fabric between Parker's legs and smell the incredible, irresistible scent of her womanhood. It was enough to make Jules want to rip the clothes right off Parker's body and devour her, but she'd promised to go slow, be gentle.

She restrained herself, hard as it was, and nudged Parker's dress up a little higher. Bare stomach, the faint outline of her ribs, the matching lace at the bottom of her bra... and then Parker pulled the dress over her head, letting it fall to the floor.

Jules bowed down, her hips resting against Parker's, and she kissed her body, from collarbone to the valley between her breasts. Then, looking up at Parker and wordlessly asking permission, she hooked a finger under the cup of her bra. Parker nodded, then Jules pulled on her bra and freed her breast. Her mouth made contact first with the delectable curve of her soft skin, inching slowly inward and placing a soft kiss right in the center of Parker's pert nipple.

She looked up at her again, her mouth still on her, and Parker had her head back, her hips pressed firmly against Jules' body, craving every touch. She couldn't resist the urge... she drew Parker's nipple into her mouth, swirling her tongue over it, memorizing the taste of her skin, thrilling at the sensation of her body tensing with pleasure beneath her.

"Oh my God," Parker breathed, squirming against Jules.

She licked and sucked and slowly made her way over to Parker's other breast, and by the time she was done, her core was aching with need.

She paused, looked up, and found Parker looking back at her.

"More," was the only word she whispered, and then she slid her hand into the tight, hot space between them, touching Jules on top of her shorts. And even with two layers of fabric between her and Parker's fingers, a shiver of pleasure ripped its way through her. Jules closed her eyes and breathed, moving herself against Parker's hand.

It had been a long, long time since anyone touched

her like that, but she'd never reacted this strongly to anyone before. Maybe it was all the waiting, all the fantasies while she told herself not to want this, but even with clothing still between them, Jules was close to the edge.

"Will you touch me?" she whispered, the words coming out pleadingly as her whole body ached shamelessly for it.

Parker nodded fervently. "I've been fantasizing about it ever since our first kiss. Show me what to do?"

"Of course," Jules said. She could feel Parker's electricity in every inch of her body and her words shot a few more volts through her.

She hurriedly tossed the couch cushions from behind her back on the floor to make more room, then stripped off her shirt and tank. Parker reached behind her back and unclipped her bra, then slid out of her panties while Jules watched. A neatly tamed tuft of dark hair crowned her slick folds, and she spread her knees apart while she waited for Jules to shed the rest of her clothes.

She was presenting herself, daring Jules to drink her in, far more boldly than Jules had expected. Jules bit her lip, trying to take in every feminine curve and delicious inch of bare skin. Then, when she was standing naked before her, Parker beckoned her with one finger.

"Come here."

Jules climbed eagerly back onto the couch, stretching out beside Parker and pulling her into her arms. Their bare breasts met, their hips interlocked, and Jules drew Parker's leg over hers to pull her closer.

They kissed, letting the tension and desire build back up between them, and then Jules took Parker's hand in hers. She kissed each one of her fingertips, licking and sucking on them as Parker reacted, and then she guided her hand down between them. She put Parker's palm against her, pressing her own hand firmly on top as she felt Parker's fingers sliding through her wetness.

She moved her hips, grinding against Parker's hand and trying to tell her body to stop. She wanted to touch Parker, come together and stare into her eyes as the pleasure took over her... but it felt so good she was having a hard time controlling herself.

"You're so wet," Parker whispered in Jules' ear, then took her earlobe into her mouth. Another shiver took her over and her body seized with the first contractions of orgasm.

Stop, she pleaded with herself, while her hips just kept moving against Parker's hand and her own, pressed together between her legs.

12

PARKER

Jules was warm and wet against her hand, and Parker pressed one finger against her entrance.

"Is this okay?" she asked. Jules nodded and rocked her hips, seating Parker's finger deeper inside her. She was hot and tight, and Parker felt a little quiver of her muscles as they contracted and squeezed her. "Wow," she breathed.

"You doing okay?" Jules asked, nuzzling Parker's neck and kissing her.

Parker pushed deeper inside Jules until she felt the hard little nub of her clit against her palm. "I'm great."

"Me too," Jules said, licking her way back up her neck and finding her mouth. Parker added a second finger and Jules moved her hips against her hand, doing most of the work while Parker got used to the incredible new sensation and the juices that were drenching her fingers.

"You feel amazing," Parker murmured as Jules' body

squeezed around her fingers again. She was getting closer and her breathing was becoming more ragged against her neck.

"So do you," Jules said, releasing Parker's hand and trailing her fingers over Parker's nipples and then down the center of her stomach. "Do you want to try to come together?"

Parker nodded fervently. Her core was already thrumming with desire, aching almost to the point of pain, but when Jules slid her hand between Parker's legs, all that pent-up energy burst like a wave crashing against a breakwater, washing over every inch of her.

Jules circled her finger around and around Parker's clit, building and ratcheting up the tension as she continued to rock her hips against Parker's hand. She slid down into her wetness and back up around her clit, plunged into her and then came back out and teased her some more. She created a symphony of sensations that had Parker seeing stars, her body tensing for the inevitable release that she was expertly teasing out of her.

If Parker was doing anything more than passively letting Jules ride her hand before, she wasn't doing it anymore, completely lost now to the unpredictable and incredibly blissful sensations between her thighs. She was so close to the edge, her vision narrowed – all she could see was Jules, the slight sheen of sweat on her temples, the gentle bounce of her small breasts as she rocked against Parker's hand.

"I'm not going to last much longer," Parker apologized, and Jules kissed her.

"That's okay," she said with a grin. "I've been trying not to come for the last five minutes. Ready?"

"Yes," Parker whined, arching her back and desperately seeking Jules' touch.

"Come with me," Jules whispered, biting down on Parker's lower lip as the rhythm of her hips turned frantic. Her finger flew over Parker's clit and she sat hard on Parker's hand, grinding her clit against her palm and crying against Parker's mouth as her climax built.

Jules came first – just a second or two before Parker – her whole body releasing and a new wave of warmth gushed between her legs, soaking Jules' hand. The sensation spurred Jules on and she redoubled her own efforts, rocking harder against Parker's hand even as her body clenched and released around her fingers. She came a second time, burying her face against the arm of the couch over Parker's shoulder as she let out a long moan and her body twitched and pulsed against Parker.

They both froze together for a moment, panting and throbbing with the aftershocks of climax, and then when she'd caught her breath, Jules collapsed beside Parker, her arms wrapped around her and one leg flung across her.

"How was it?" she asked.

"I'm speechless," Parker told her.

Jules laughed. "That bad, huh?"

Parker lifted her head to look into Jules' eyes. "I never knew I could come that hard. And watching you come... holy shit, that was hot."

Jules captured her mouth in her own then, kissing her passionately and beginning to move her hips against Parker's with the first cravings of renewed lust. When she released her, she asked, "Want to take a shower, maybe try it again? There are plenty of other tricks I could teach you to make you come even harder."

She wiggled her tongue at Parker, who blushed and felt her core growing hot all at the same time. She got up off the couch and held her hand out to Jules, pulling her to her feet. "So, is this a pretty average first date for you?"

Jules chuckled. "You know, my memory is pretty fuzzy because it's been a minute since my last first date, but I can't think of a better one."

Parker turned and walked backward a few paces, not letting go of Jules' hand. "Is it safe to say there's gonna be a second date?"

"Who says this one has to end?" Jules asked, following her up the stairs.

In the morning the next day, Jules and Parker came downstairs to find Lucky's pen open and the little brown bunny nowhere to be found.

"Oh no," Parker groaned. "I never put Lucky away last night."

"Be prepared for chewed baseboards and scratched floors," Jules said as they looked for the rabbit.

"I hope not," Parker said. "Wait, here he is!"

Lucky was sprawled on top of one of the couch cushions they'd thrown to the floor the night before, his ears perked up as he acknowledged their arrival. Parker looked all over but there weren't any signs of destruction – not even a stray poop outside Lucky's litterbox.

"What a good boy you are," she said, scooping him up and giving him a kiss on the tip of his nose. "I'm just going to put him back in his pen then out to the barn and give everybody else breakfast."

"Okay," Jules said. "Mind if I make coffee?"

"Help yourself," Parker said. She walked outside barefoot, feeling a strange mix of tired and energized and trying to process everything that had happened the night before.

Before their date, she'd thought about kissing Jules again, and about what it might feel like to go further. She'd even fantasized about being with her, touching her, but she didn't expect things to get so hot and heavy so fast, or for it to feel so good, or to come so naturally to her.

Her body just fit with Jules' and she loved every minute of exploring the way they connected, the way Jules made her feel and the way Jules reacted when Parker touched her.

By the time she got back into the house, the kitchen was filled with the welcome aroma of coffee and Parker couldn't get the damn smile off her face.

"You look happy this morning," Jules said, handing her a cup.

"I am," Parker said. "Are you?"

"Very," Jules said, then smirked and added, "I'm quite satisfied."

Parker dropped her chin, looking through her lashes

at Jules as she teased her, saying, "Darn, and I was hoping for a quickie before you have to leave for work."

Jules consulted the clock on the wall and winked at her. "I think that can be arranged. You're insatiable, Miss Rose."

Parker set her coffee down, forgetting all about it as Jules encircled her in her arms. They kissed, then she said, "I came here sort of at the end of my rope, hoping that I could be happy and successful here but with no real expectations. But it turns out this is right where I needed to be all along. It feels like coming up for air after a very long time underwater."

Jules kissed her again, wrapping those firm biceps around her in an embrace that felt comfortingly possessive.

When they pulled apart again, Parker said, "You know I would never intentionally let Lucky chew the baseboards and destroy your parents' house, right?"

"I know," Jules said, sliding one finger along Parker's forehead and tucking a strand of hair behind her ear. "But it's not my parents' house anymore – it's yours. At least it will be in another six weeks. You can paint the whole place Day-Glo green for all I care. Turn the basement into a sex dungeon."

Parker laughed. "Are you into that?"

"Right now, I'm just into you," Jules said. "I do have a dog neutering appointment in about three hours so unfortunately I will need to leave eventually, but what do you say we continue our first date this evening? I can take you to get that ice cream I teased you with yesterday."

"Yummy," Parker said, licking her lips. "I'm game."

Over the next couple of weeks, the never-ending first date expanded to include ice cream, strawberry picking, swimming in the little man-made lake east of town, mini golf, eating at every restaurant Camden had to offer, playing with rabbits – of course – and a complete review of every sapphic-leaning movie Netflix had to offer.

One lazy Sunday afternoon, with *But I'm a Cheerleader* playing in the background, Parker sat cross-legged on the couch. Lucky was in her lap and they were both watching Jules dig around in a closet.

"He's a little cuddler," she said, putting her hand back on Lucky's head after she'd stopped for just a second and he'd looked at her like a great offense had been committed.

"He loves you," Jules said. "You saved him."

"I love him too," Parker said. "Hey, what are you doing?"

"Looking for this," Jules said, coming out of the coat closet triumphantly with a little plastic storage container. "It must have gotten buried when I was clearing the clutter before you got here."

"What is it?"

Jules joined her on the couch and Lucky appraised her, trying to decide who was going to provide the better petting – and possibly treats. Jules pulled the coffee table closer and busied herself with the container, so Lucky stuck with Parker.

"It's my mish-mash of art supplies," Jules explained, dumping a collection of colored pencils, markers, sequins, pipe cleaners, and all sorts of other random items onto the table.

Parker laughed, picking up a googly eye the size of a quarter and setting it on top of Lucky's head. "And what should we do with these? Give Lucky a third eye and see if he can attain enlightenment?"

"Maybe later," Jules said. "But in the meantime, I thought we could make him a name tag — you're not an official Wakefield rescue rabbit until you've got a name tag."

She picked up a piece of cardstock and held a handful of markers out to Parker.

"Wanna help?"

"I thought name tags were your thing," Parker said. "I wouldn't want to break with tradition."

"Let's make a new tradition," Jules said, leaning in to kiss her, then handing her a marker.

Parker took it, then greedily stole another kiss. Lucky, apparently fearing for his life while being squished between them, hopped down to the floor, so Jules scooted a little closer. They spent the next twenty minutes pouring all their love and attention into creating Lucky's name tag, which ended up a mosaic of shamrocks and hearts. Even Lucky contributed, jumping back onto the couch after a few minutes and venturing onto the coffee table to take a nibble out of the corner of the card.

"A masterpiece," Parker declared as soon as they were done. "I don't know if I can bear to send him out to the barn after all this time inside though."

Jules gave her a knowing smile and said, "I kinda figured you would get attached to this little guy. Here."

She got up and used one of the pipe cleaners to hang the name tag from the front of the pen in the living room where Lucky had been staying while his ear mite infestation cleared up.

"There," she said. "He's a house bunny now."

Being with Jules felt like the difference between night and day when Parker thought back to what it had been like with David, even in the beginning.

Where he was self-centered and demanding of Parker's time, Jules liked to go with the flow. Where David needed everything to revolve around him, Jules lavished her attention on Parker. And where he took what he wanted in bed and rolled over to go to sleep, assuming that Parker was satisfied too, Jules took her time, making sure Parker fell asleep exhausted and happy.

And of course, Parker had to tell her best friend about all these new developments – if not the intimate details. One day when Jules was at work and Parker was waiting for a batch of treats to come out of the oven, she and Kani were chatting online.

ParksAndWreck: Sometimes I wonder if I even knew what love felt like before Jules.

KaniConeja: WAIT wait wait wait wait

ParksAndWreck: Umm... yes?

KaniConeja: Did you just say you love Jules?

ParksAndWreck: ...no? I don't know! I just said I don't know what love is.

KaniConeja: You just said you DIDN'T know what love felt like

ParksAndWreck: Are you secretly a lawyer with all these semantics? Because I gotta say, after David, that profession is a real turn-off for me.

KaniConeja: Doesn't matter to me – I'm not the one you're in love with

ParksAndWreck: Stop.

KaniConeja: But it's true, isn't it?

ParksAndWreck: The oven timer's going off – give me five.

KaniConeja: A likely story...

After that, Parker tried to be a little more careful with her words when she was talking to Kani. First, she'd planted the ear worm that made Parker question her sexuality, and now this... Kani was a Level 5 Wizard when it came to getting inside Parker's head in the worst way.

That thought – *how do you REALLY know that you love someone?* – was floating through the back of Parker's mind as she and Jules drove out of Camden one evening on their way to the drive-in movie theater one town over.

"Hey," Jules said, reaching across the bench seat and taking Parker's hand. "You have a rough day?"

"Hmm? No, why?"

"You just seem a little... introspective."

"Oh," Parker said. "I was just thinking about an adoption appointment that's coming up for Bugs. Can't wait for the movie, though – I've never been on an actual date to a drive-in."

"Well, I can't say it gets as steamy in real life as it does in the movies, but we *do* have an entire cooler full of snacks," Jules said with a wink.

"You had me at snacks," Parker said, but they never actually made it to the drive-in.

When they were about ten minutes outside of Camden, Jules' phone started ringing and she checked the caller ID, then frowned. "It's one of my vet friends, Sydney. She usually only calls at this hour if it's work-related – mind if I take this?"

"Not at all," Parker said, then she watched Jules'

expression change from curiosity to concern while she spoke.

"Hey, Syd, what's up?... Oh no... Where is it?... Yeah, I'm about ten minutes away from there... Just a sec, let me ask." She turned to Parker. "There's a deer caught in a wrought iron fence a few miles from here and Sydney's trying to get it out, but it's panicking and she's worried it may break its neck trying to wrench itself free. Do you mind if we—"

"Not at all," Parker said. "We can go to the movies any time."

"Thank you," Jules said, leaning across the seat to give her a quick kiss before bringing the phone back up to her ear. "Syd? We'll be there soon – hang on."

She hung up and did a quick U-turn, then headed down a less-traveled country road that ran perpendicular to the main road out of Camden. She pressed down on the gas and while they drove, Parker asked, "Do you get that sort of call often?"

"No, but Sydney does," Jules said. "She works for a wildlife rehab center and they get calls like this all the time. Usually one of her coworkers will respond if she needs help, but the center is about an hour from here and they take calls all over the state. If the animal is in distress and she needs backup, she calls whatever vet in her network is closest. In this area, that's me."

"You are truly an amazing, compassionate woman, Jules Wakefield," Parker said. "And you surprise me every day."

"I'm just doing my job," Jules objected.

"That's the point," Parker told her. "You've dedicated your life to helping animals.

"So have you," Jules pointed out. "Anyway, thanks for not minding about the movie. I can't promise this is the only time it'll ever happen – such is the life of a small-town vet."

"There'll be other showings," Parker said. "Animal welfare comes first, obviously." Then she looked at the cooler between her feet and added with a laugh, "Besides, I'd be lying if I said it hadn't occurred to me to go home and feed you snacks where things *can* get steamy."

When Jules and Parker arrived at the address Sydney had given, a big pickup truck with an animal transport cage on the back was already waiting.

Jules asked Parker, "Do you want to wait in the truck?"

"No way," Parker said. "I helped you birth those kids – you know I'm not afraid of getting my hands dirty. I'll help if I can."

"Okay," Jules said. "But stay alert – if it's a buck, those horns can be lethal, especially when it's scared."

Parker and Jules got out of the truck. They were at a large house in a rural neighborhood where grass grew instead of crops, and all the houses were enormous and pretty far apart. There was a tall iron fence surrounding the entire property, and there was just enough daylight left in the sky to make out a couple of shadowy figures near the back corner of the house.

"That must be Syd," Jules said, raising a hand.

The figure repeated the gesture, so Jules and Parker followed the fence at a jog, slowing down before they got too close to avoid spooking the deer.

"Oh no," Parker breathed when she saw it. It was indeed a buck, with his head tilted sideways and one antler thoroughly tangled in the vertical bars of the fence. "How did you even get like that, buddy?"

"It's just lucky he's not injured – I've seen 'em misjudge the height of these fences plenty of times and those spikes at the top aren't decorative," the woman standing a little bit away from the deer said. She was tall, with pin-straight hair pulled back in a long ponytail down her back, and she wore thick coveralls despite the heat.

"This is Sydney," Jules said. "Syd, my... girlfriend, Parker."

She paused on the word, looking to Parker as if checking to see if it was okay. Parker smiled, and Jules had the biggest grin on her face before she turned back to Sydney.

"She's not a vet but she takes direction well if we need another hand," she added.

"Good to meet ya, Parker," Sydney said, giving her a wave because she was too far away for a handshake – and besides, Parker figured the deer wouldn't want to wait around for them all to become best friends before they freed him.

"What's the game plan?" Jules asked.

"I don't want to have to cut the bars," Sydney said. "It'll scare the hell out of him, and the homeowners'll be pissed if they come outside and find a big hole in their expensive fence."

"Anybody home?" Jules asked, and Sydney nodded.

"They're the ones who called. I told them to stay inside because they have a bunch of kids and I didn't want them freaking the buck out any more than he already is."

"What if we get them to let Parker in so she can stand on the other side of the fence and try to keep him calm?" Jules suggested. "At the very least, she'll be something distracting for him to focus on while we try to get him free on this side."

Sydney nodded. "Sounds as good as any plan I've got. You okay with that, hon?"

Parker nodded and jogged back up the length of the fence as quick as she could. She buzzed at the gate and used the intercom to explain the plan to the woman who answered. The gate swung open and Parker ran back up the inside of the fence.

The deer's nose was pressed uncomfortably against the fence and there was a look of wild terror in his eyes. Parker made a tentative move to reach out to him and his eyes only got wider so she stopped.

"It's okay," she cooed. "We're here to help you." She looked up at Jules and Sydney. "Am I okay here?"

"Yeah," Sydney said. "Just do whatever you can to keep his attention on you so he doesn't panic and start thrashing around when we come closer."

Parker nodded, her heart climbing into her throat as she got as close to the fence as she dared. She was perfectly safe where she was, but her eyes went to the sharp points of the buck's antlers and she could barely breathe as Jules inched closer to him from behind.

"It'll all be over in a minute," Parker promised the deer. "You got yourself in a pickle but your friendly neighborhood vets are here to help you out of it."

"Pull to the right," Sydney said quietly and Jules quickly fell into place.

They grabbed the deer's antlers and maneuvered, giving each other directions as they tried to puzzle out how to free him. Parker kept talking, trying to be as soothing as possible, but inside, her pulse was racing. One wrong move with those pointy antlers and…

"Push him upward, go!" Sydney said and in an instant, the deer was free. The two of them flattened themselves against the fence, out of his way, and then he was bounding through the grass toward a tree line in the distance.

Parker collapsed forward, catching the bars of the fence in her hands and feeling the cool metal against her face as adrenaline dumped into her veins. "Is he going to be okay?"

"Yeah, as long as he doesn't repeat his mistakes," Sydney said. "Thanks for your help – both of you."

Jules turned toward Parker, kissing her through the fence. "You were great."

"Thanks," Parker said. "So were you – and you, Sydney. That was amazing."

"All in a day's work," Sydney said. She obviously subscribed to the same Modesty School of Veterinary Heroism that Jules was a member of, and she said goodbye then drove down to the intercom to fill the homeowners in on what happened.

While Parker and Jules walked back down to the truck, on opposite sides of the fence, Parker checked the time on her phone. "That didn't take long. I bet we could still make the movie."

"We could go if you want to," Jules said, "but now I'm intrigued at that *eating snacks and getting amorous* idea you had earlier."

Parker laughed. "Whatever you say, *girlfriend.*"

13

JULES

"Are you *sure* it's okay?" Parker asked for what seemed like the hundredth time. She was standing behind Jules at the kitchen table and she had her arms wrapped around her. She was talking about having her parents come to visit.

"Yes," Jules said. "I told you so. Come here." She tugged on Parker's hand and pulled her into the chair beside her, dragging it across the tile floor so their knees were intertwined. "I want you to feel at home here because this *is* your home. I don't want you to feel like you can't have guests – especially your parents – just because..."

She trailed off. *Because mine are dead.*

Even though every successive day was getting just a little bit easier, it was never truly easy to talk about. The fact that summer was turning into fall and the anniversaries of the worst two days of her life were rapidly approaching didn't do anything to help matters.

She'd actually let Marissa set up the timing of the contest to end on the same week that her parents passed – Jules had told her to schedule it as soon as possible, and that was just how it worked out. She convinced herself at the time that it wouldn't be a big deal, and she was hoping that by the time she and Parker got to week twelve, it really wouldn't be.

"Babe," she said, "I know you're close to your parents and that's beautiful, and if you've been putting off their visit just to protect my feelings, I'm sorry. I want you to see them. And I want them to see what an incredible job you're doing here."

"Okay, I'll let them know," Parker said. She leaned in closer and rested her forehead against Jules'. "And you can meet them if you're ready, but there's no pressure."

She *did* want to meet Parker's parents. From everything she'd heard, they sounded like wonderful people, and they'd have to be to raise a woman like Parker.

She'd been happily referring to Parker as her girlfriend whenever she got the chance over the last few weeks and the two of them spent every spare minute together. But meeting the parents? What would it feel like to see Parker interacting with them, to hear stories from Parker's childhood, to watch them hug her when Jules' parents could never do that again? What if they were *too much* like her own parents and it just hurt too much?

"I'd like to meet them," she said honestly. "But I don't know if I'm ready."

"I understand," Parker said, nudging Jules with her

nose until she raised her head, then kissing her. "It's okay."

"Thank you."

"Now," Parker said, pulling Jules out of the chair and giving her a swat on the behind, "I've got rabbits to feed and treats to bake, and you've got to get to the clinic."

Jules checked the time – a quarter to eight. She'd been spending a lot of nights here with Parker and there was something really special about being able to wake up next to her, tug the sheets down and admire her bare breasts in the morning sun, come downstairs and have a lazy morning sipping coffee and chatting before they each went on their way. Jules hadn't felt so content in a long time.

Parker's parents came to town a week later and planned to stay for the weekend. Jules was on the fence about meeting them the entire time they waited together for Parker's parents to take the bus down, and in the meantime, something curious was happening online.

"Look, another order!" Parker said from her spot on the glider beside Jules. She held up her phone to show her – sure enough, the rabbit treat and birthday cake orders had been pouring into her Etsy shop. "I'm up to six just today. That's a record."

"That's amazing, babe," Jules said, giving her a big, celebratory kiss. "I'm proud of you."

Parker laughed. "I'm not sure what for – I haven't done anything different."

"Is it word of mouth?" Jules asked. "Maybe your friends on Bunny Central have been talking you up?"

Jules had never actually spoken to Parker's friend, Kani, but the impression she got of her was of a well-intentioned and caring busybody. She wouldn't put it past Kani to do some marketing work on the sly to help Parker boost her business. Parker had set up a small display in the reception area at the clinic and it had generated a few orders, but it couldn't account for this volume.

"I don't think so," Parker said. "At least not more than usual. I get a couple orders a week from people on the forum."

She frowned and thought for a little while, and another order came in.

"Seven!" she exclaimed.

"You're going viral," Jules teased. "Soon you're gonna have to find a manufacturer to help you handle all those orders."

"But then they wouldn't be *handmade with love* like my shop says," Parker told her.

They spent the afternoon on the screened-in porch, with Lucky, Jack, and a few other bunnies hopping around their feet and exploring the space. By the time Parker needed to drive into Granville and pick her parents up at the bus depot, she was up to ten orders in her queue and Jules still hadn't given her a definitive answer about whether she was up for meeting her parents this weekend.

As Parker got up from the glider, Jules felt a tightening in her chest. "I don't think I can do it," she said. "I'm sorry. I want to—"

"Don't say another word," Parker said. "Please, don't worry about it. My parents want to meet you but I told them you get busy with work a lot and there's no expectation – either from them or from me. You'll meet them when you're ready."

"Thank you," Jules said. "You go, and drive safely. I'll corral the bunnies and head back to my apartment."

"Okay," Parker said, leaning in for a kiss. "Thank you."

She started to head for the door but Jules grabbed her hand and spun her back. She put her truck keys in Parker's hand. "Take my truck. That ancient Geo's fine for driving around town but I don't like the idea of you breaking down and getting stranded in between Camden and Granville."

Parker laughed. "Now I'm *sure* you and my mother will get along when you meet because she said the same thing to me when I first got here."

"Smart woman," Jules said.

"What about you? How are you going to get to town without your truck?" Parker asked, and Jules shrugged.

"I'll walk. It's only five miles."

Parker laughed and handed Jules her keys. "Take the Geo, since you're such a big fan. I'm going to take my parents to Norie's Place for dinner – if you want to come, just call."

"Okay," Jules said.

She walked with Parker around the front of the house and watched her climb into the pickup, then disappear down the road. Then Jules went back inside the house, feeling slightly odd being there alone, and caught all the bunnies and brought them back to the barn stalls where they belonged.

She paused there for a few minutes, marveling at how many new faces she saw. Parker had been busy in her first two and a half months here. She'd placed a lot of the original two dozen that Jules had handed over to her care, and taken in plenty of new bunnies. There were eighteen of them in the barn right now, and Jules paused when she got to the end of the row and saw Cotton in her stall.

"Hey, girl," Jules said, resting her forearms on the top of the stall door and glancing at the hastily made name tag that she'd decorated months ago, back when she didn't have time to breathe, let alone make decent name tags. Cotton raised onto her back feet to look at her. "Still waiting for your fur-ever home, huh?"

The white rabbits with pink eyes were always difficult to adopt out – as well as the ones that had all-black coats, which people were superstitious about. They were always the last to be picked. Jules had learned that sad fact through observation in her years of watching her parents match rabbits to adoptive families. And from what Parker told her, Cotton wasn't helping her case much.

She was such a rambunctious little Houdini that she made the whole process ten times harder than it had to be. During appointments with potential adopters, she'd dig at the carpet in the living room, nip little children's fingers when she mistook them for carrots, and race around like a wild thing no matter how much exercise Parker tried to give her beforehand to tire her out.

She was a sweet little cuddle bunny once she got used to people, but so far, no one but Parker and Jules could get close enough for that to happen.

Jules reached into the stall to stroke Cotton's ears and said, "Don't worry – your family's out there somewhere. You just gotta be patient… and a little better behaved."

She closed up the barn and climbed into the driver's seat of Parker's little Geo. It was surprisingly roomy inside for its size, but that didn't change the number of holes that years of rust had eaten into its body panels and Jules felt better knowing Parker was in her sturdy truck.

Jules drove back to her apartment above the clinic, feeling a little bit like a coward on the retreat, and tried to prepare for a weekend alone – something she hadn't done in weeks. Parker was right – this wouldn't last forever and someday, hopefully soon, she'd feel up to meeting a new set of parents. For now, though, she sank into her couch, turned on Netflix and tried to ignore the feeling of disappointment that kept nagging at her.

*J*ules woke with a start.

Something was buzzing urgently against her hip and when she looked outside, it was light but she didn't know if it was still light out on Friday evening, or already light on Saturday morning. How long had she been sleeping?

She fumbled for her phone and saw Parker's name. "H'lo?"

"Hey, babe," Parker said, extra chipper. "Were you asleep?"

Jules looked at the TV. It was in the middle of an episode of *Buffy* and the judgmental 'Are you still watching?' screen hadn't even popped up yet, so it must still be Friday. She just fell asleep for a little while, a quick nap. She sat up and muted the TV, saying, "Yeah, but I'm up now. Is everything okay? Are you back?"

"We're driving back now," Parker said. "But you'll never guess what happened."

"Oh no," Jules said, her mind automatically going negative. "The truck didn't break down, did it? I just had it serviced—"

"No, it's nothing bad!" Parker said. "Remember how I was getting all those orders earlier?"

"Yeah, did you figure out why?"

"I did, and I got a *whole bunch* more orders," Parker said. "I checked my email while I was waiting for Mom and Dad's bus and I got a message from Etsy – they featured my shop on the front page, and rabbit owners are sharing it all over social media. I really am going viral."

"Oh my God, Parker, that's amazing!" Jules said, completely alert now. "I'm so excited for you!"

"Me too," Parker said. "There is one problem though."

"What is it?"

"I have over a hundred orders in my queue right now," she said. "That would take me all weekend even if I didn't have my parents here. I'm going to have to message all these people and tell them I need more time to deliver—"

"You can't do that, doodlebug," Jules heard a woman's voice say in the background. *"Not when you're just getting all this attention. If you need to bake this weekend, we understand."*

"Sure do, bug," a man's voice added. Jules smiled. Parker's parents sounded sweet, supportive.

"It's not just the time," Parker told them. "It'd literally take me all weekend working by myself—"

"How long would it take with three extra sets of hands?" Jules cut in.

Parker paused for a second. "You… want to help?"

"Am I on speakerphone?" Jules asked.

"No," Parker said.

"I've been wanting to watch you work for a while now," she said. "I bet it's really sexy – you in an apron, with your hair up in a messy bun, working up a sweat in the kitchen and being a hot boss babe." She imagined Parker's cheeks reddening and a little spark of desire awoke in her core. Then, because she knew Parker's parents were squeezed into the truck cab beside her, she let up and added more casually, "Besides, you've helped me with my work – I wanna return the favor, and I'm sure your parents wouldn't mind being put to work for one night."

"Are you okay with..." Parker trailed off. Jules knew she probably didn't want to say *meeting my parents* in earshot of them, lest they get the wrong idea about Jules' reluctance, but she got the message anyway.

"Yeah," she said. "I think this is good, actually. Making treats will give us all something to focus on and I won't be able to get inside my head like I would if we were just going out to dinner or something. I really do wanna help, Parker."

"That means a lot to me," she said. "Mom, Dad—"

"We'd be happy to help," the woman's voice said. *"Put us to work, bug."*

"What do you need me to do?" Jules asked. "Should I stop at the grocery store and pick up ingredients?"

Parker gave her a list over the phone – which included more bananas than Jules had ever purchased in one shopping trip before – and then she gave her an ETA. She and her parents were about forty-five minutes outside of Camden, which gave Jules just enough time to place a pizza order, get over to the grocery store, and head back out to the farmhouse.

Her truck was already in the driveway when Jules arrived, and a tall, slightly portly man with gray hair and a kind smile came outside when she pulled up.

"You must be the famous Jules," he said, extending a hand. "I'm Parker's dad, Mark."

"It's nice to meet you," Jules said, taking his hand. He was tall like her own father had been, and she could see warmth in his eyes, but luckily he didn't physically resemble her dad in any other way.

She put the thought out of her head as Mark said, "Parker and her mom are in the kitchen greasing pans and getting everything ready. They sent me out here to help carry groceries, so load me up."

"Thanks," Jules said, pointing to the back seat of the Geo. "Can you grab those bags? I got us a couple of pizzas and a two-liter for dinner."

"Sounds great," Mark said. "That six-hour bus ride felt more like ten – I'm starved."

Jules grabbed the pizzas off the passenger seat and Mark followed her inside with the rest of the bags. They went into the kitchen, which Parker had indeed turned into her command center. There were mixing bowls lining the countertop and a half-dozen sheet pans on the table, along with some silicone molds and round cookie cutters.

"Wow," Jules said as she looked around for a flat, unclaimed surface to set down the pizzas. "This really does look like a factory."

"I'm up to a hundred and twenty orders," Parker said, clearing a space for Jules and then throwing her arms around her. "Thanks for helping – I honestly don't know how long it'd take if I had to do all this by myself."

"Happy to," Jules said.

"Oh, this is my mom!" Parker said, turning to make the introductions. "Mom, Jules. Jules, my mother, Patricia."

"It's nice to meet you," Jules said, holding out her hand, but Parker's mom ignored it and pulled her into a hug instead.

"I've heard so much about you," she said. "I was upset at first, when my daughter told me she was moving a whole state away right after I'd gotten her back, but I can't argue with the results. She's like a whole new girl, with you to thank."

"Mom," Parker objected, looking a little embarrassed.

Her mom waved a hand at her and added, "And please, call me Patty."

Jules looked from Parker to her parents, both beaming and proud of her for the life she'd built here in the last few months. She knew they talked on the phone often, and that Parker and her mom were close, just like Jules used to be with her own mother.

She told her everything, including the confusing, excited way she'd felt when they first kissed, and the fact that they were dating now. And Parker's parents had been supportive every step of the way, just like Jules' parents had been when she came out to them in high school – a minor miracle, especially for small-town folks.

"I brought dinner," Jules said, then looked over to find Mark already helping himself.

"Sorry," he said with his cheeks stuffed. "Hungry."

Jules chuckled – it was totally something her own dad would have done, and much to her relief, it didn't hurt at all to realize that. She went over to the cabinets and retrieved enough plates and cups for everyone and they ate while Parker talked them through the game plan.

She was confident and organized, rising to the occasion beautifully... and she really did have her hair up in a messy bun that was sexy as hell. As she watched Parker move about the kitchen, a half-eaten slice of pizza in one hand and explaining her treat recipe, Jules thought, *I think I love her.*

14

PARKER

"Congratulations on a job well done, Miss Entrepreneur," Jules said, drawing Parker closer to her in the nest of sheets they'd made for themselves on the floor.

There was a mile-long receipt full of tracking codes from the post office downstairs on the kitchen table and Parker's bank account was no longer dwindling in the triple digits. There were more orders filling her Etsy queue every day and a variety of rabbit-oriented websites and social media groups had been sharing her shop all weekend.

She'd have to keep going full steam ahead to fill those orders and Jules had even suggested that she should hire part-time help to give her a hand.

"My vet tech, Shawn, has a teenage daughter," she'd said while Parker, Jules and Parker's parents finished packaging the massive batch of treats they'd made on

Friday night. "I've known her since she was in pigtails and she'd be a hard worker."

"I just can't believe my silly little side project has gotten so big I'm thinking about hiring an employee," Parker had said at the time, and it didn't feel any less surreal now.

The four of them had filled all one hundred and twenty orders that Parker got on Friday, and they'd needed Jules' truck to take all the boxes to the post office on Saturday morning. They spent a full hour there mailing them all out, but after that, Parker changed her expected shipping times on all new orders to give herself the rest of the weekend off. She got to spend quality time with her parents, showing them around the rescue and the farmhouse and giving them the same tour of Camden that Jules had given her.

And Jules stuck around all weekend, quickly getting over her concerns about her own parents and getting to know Parker's. It meant a lot to her, and as soon as her parents were safely back on the bus to Illinois, Parker dragged Jules to bed to show her appreciation.

They'd made love once already on Sunday night, so passionately that at one point Jules rolled over and fell right off the bed. Parker had sat up, laughing at Jules with her back on the floor and her feet still on the mattress, and Jules retaliated by grabbing Parker and pulling her down to the floor with her, sheets and all.

Now, they lay together with the sheets twisted around their naked limbs and Jules ran her hand over

Parker's hair, brushing it out of her face and playing with the silky tendrils.

"Your parents are really nice," she said. "I'm glad you have them, and that they support you like they do."

Parker's heart was full. She'd always loved her parents and knew she was lucky to have them, but she'd never truly appreciated them like she did this weekend. When the emotion threatened to bring tears to her eyes, she smacked Jules' shoulder and said, "Don't talk about my parents while we're naked."

Jules nudged the sheet down, exposing Parker's breast, and gave her a surprised look. "So we are. Hmm... what to do?"

She brought her mouth down to Parker's nipple, closing her lips around it and sending a spark of electricity all the way through her body and down into her core.

"That's a start," Parker said, reaching beneath the sheets and finding Jules' wetness. Jules spread her thighs for her and Parker buried her fingers deep in her, making Jules moan and then bringing her fingers to her mouth, tasting the spoils of her last climax.

She'd been a little nervous the first time she and Jules made love because it was entirely new territory for her, and she'd been nervous to go out and hold hands with her around Camden because she knew people could be mean and ignorant sometimes, and back then, Parker hadn't quite processed the way Jules made her feel.

But everyone here was so warm and accepting, of Parker and of her newfound status as Jules' girlfriend. If anything, it seemed like the people of Camden were happy to see Jules with someone making her happy after a long period of loneliness.

Now, Parker was never nervous about touching Jules, kissing her, licking her, tasting her juices, opening herself up to let Jules do all of the above to her in return, and curling up in her arms afterward. It felt so good, so perfect.

She started to crawl down between Jules' thighs, eager to lap up her sweetness right from the source, but Jules stopped her. Parker looked into her eyes, confused at first, thinking there was something wrong. But instead she saw that Jules' face was positively flooded with emotion. Her eyes sparkled, her cheeks were pink, her mouth curved up in a subtle, secret smile.

"What?" Parker asked.

Jules brought her hands up to Parker's face, cupping her cheeks and keeping her gaze locked on her. "I love you, Parker."

Parker's lips parted. She'd been falling for Jules since she'd arrived and those three words had gone through her head a multitude of times lately. Whenever they were together, it seemed like the words were pressing at the back of her teeth, begging to come out.

But right in this moment, now that Jules had actually given voice to them, Parker's breath caught in her throat and she was speechless. After a moment, she managed, "You do?"

"Yes," Jules said earnestly. Then she broke into a grin and her hands went down to Parker's hips, guiding her as she said, "Now sit on my face so I can show you how much."

Before Parker had a chance to untie her tongue, Jules had maneuvered her backward and on top of her, guiding her hips down over her mouth. Parker opened her own mouth, intending to return the favor, but instead Jules' tongue found her clit and all that came out was a long, shivery moan.

She gave up on talking and laid down along Jules' length, enjoying the feeling of their bodies pressed together as Jules lapped at her and Parker rubbed her hand in long, languid strokes up and down through Jules' wetness.

It didn't take long for Parker to come – Jules knew just how to touch her and tease her and bring her to the brink. Her body tensed, then exploded into a thousand little fires as Jules hungrily lapped at her release.

Parker rolled to the side, wrapping her arm around Jules' thigh and bringing her hips along for the ride. She buried her face between her legs and plunged her fingers deep into Jules' wetness. Working her hand and her tongue in unison, she had Jules writhing and coming beneath her in no time, and when they were both spent for the moment, Parker crawled back up and laid down beside her.

She wiped her mouth, giving Jules a big, satisfied grin, then said, "I love you too."

Jules pounced on her, pinning her to the bed before she rained kisses down in the general vicinity of her mouth, saying, "That's only because I just made you come."

Parker caught her in her arms, pulling Jules down to snuggle against her, and their kisses turned slower, more sensual. "And I appreciate that, but no, that's not why. I've been thinking it for a while now."

"So have I," Jules said. She settled into the crook of Parker's arm, a few wisps of her short hair sticking up at odd angles and tickling Parker's nose, but she didn't care – she'd lay there forever with Jules if she could.

She did love her – of that, Parker was certain. But she'd never truly been loved back until this moment. And that meant there was something Parker had to do.

The next day, after Jules left to open the clinic, Parker logged into Bunny Central and looked for Kani. Luckily, she was online and Parker sent her a message.

ParksAndWreck: Got a minute?

KaniConeja: For you, Brad? I've got five

ParksAndWreck: Ooh... Kevin Spacey quotes are so 2016. Regardless, I'm gonna Skype you in a minute.

A couple minutes later, thanks to the marvels of modern technology and a surprisingly fast internet connection in the middle of the soybean fields, Parker was watching her best friend polish off a piece of *ruisleipä*, a type of rye bread that she'd once sent to Parker in a care package that was surprisingly tasty even after a transatlantic trip.

"Dinner time?" Parker guessed, doing the math in her head and realizing it was a little past four p.m. in Finland.

"Snack before studying," Kani said, her cheeks stuffed. "So what's up?"

"Jules and I said *I love you*," Parker told her. "Yesterday, for the first time."

Kani's eyes went big and she dropped the *ruisleipä*. "YOU DID?"

Parker laughed. "Yes."

"Tell me, tell me!" Kani demanded. "I want details."

"Well, uh, we were naked at the time so I can't really give you details," Parker said, blushing as she thought back to the way Jules had hauled her around by her hips and planted her right where she wanted her. "But Kani, we've only got two more weeks before the trial period for the rescue ends and now that I know she loves me, and I love her... I have to tell her."

Kani rolled her eyes. "Not this again. I thought you were past it."

"I tried to forget about it like you said," Parker told her. "But I can't get it out of my head. It's not right to let her sign the property over to me under false pretenses, and I can't keep telling her that I love her knowing there's this big secret that I'm keeping from her."

"It's not a big secret!" Kani argued. "It's a little one –

a tiny detail, a technicality, even. I wrote your contest essay – so what?"

"So, I never really applied to be here!"

"But you wanted to be."

"But I didn't take the initiative," Parker argued. "Jules wanted someone who would do that."

"What have you done since you got there?" Kani challenged. "How many rabbits have you placed in forever homes?"

"Thirteen," Parker answered.

"And how many more have you taken in, all without asking for a dime or being a burden to Jules?"

"Seven."

"Do you think she really loves you for who you are? And do you both enjoy being with each other?"

"Yes," Parker said. "Yes, I do."

"And do you think she would have just fallen in love with *anyone* who won the contest and moved into her parents' house?"

"No, of course not."

"*It's fate, Parker,*" Kani insisted. "I wrote your essay because *somebody* had to write it – the gods act in mysterious ways but they're not corporeal, they can't hold pens or use the internet."

Parker couldn't help stifling a laugh at that, but Kani caught it and smiled.

"You're exactly where you ought to be and you're making a mountain out of a molehill," Kani said. When Parker frowned, unconvinced, Kani read that on her face too and added, "Do you want to know what I think you're really doing?"

"What?"

"Trying to push her away."

"What? No," Parker objected. "I just told you we said *I love you—*"

"And that probably scares the hell out of you after David," Kani said. "Don't you think it's a little convenient that everything's been going great for weeks, and all of a sudden it's two weeks from the day you're going to take ownership of the rescue and really cement your life there, and *now* you want to do something that could blow it all sky high?"

"But—"

"Answer the question, Parks."

"Yeah, okay," she said grudgingly. "It's convenient timing, and maybe I am scared. I had no intention of getting into a relationship out here. I didn't even *really* think about what it would be like to move here permanently – I just needed someplace to go and you and Jules were handing me the rescue on a platter. And now I'm in love with a woman – really, deeply in love with her, Kani – and I still feel like I don't quite know what love *means.*"

"You don't have to define it," Kani said. "You just have to do it."

"How does one *do* love?"

Kani shrugged. "Okay, fine, you don't do it, you make it. You build it. You do everything in your power to make your partner happy, knowing that they make you happy, and above all, you never give up on it. You fight for it because it's the most precious thing we have. Don't throw it away, Parks."

Parker smiled. "Since when did you get so sappy and sentimental?"

Kani grinned. "Phillies girl brings it out of me."

"Oh yeah?" Parker said. "That's going well?"

Kani just nodded, and now it was Parker's turn to pry more information out of her. While Kani gushed about her new love interest, whose name was Lana, Parker looked around the living room. All of Jules' family photos still hung on the walls. She never did ask to collect them, and now that she was spending so much time at the farmhouse, it didn't make sense to take them all down.

But the anniversaries of their deaths were coming up. Jules almost never talked about it and Parker didn't press her, but she'd learned the dates from Hannah once when they were at Norie's Place, and she wanted to do something nice for Jules to help her get through those days.

"There's something I've got to do, Kani," she said. "I'll let you get back to your *ruisleipä*... and your Phillies girl."

Kani laughed. "Your Finnish pronunciation is still terrible. We'll have to work on that."

15

JULES

"Why in God's name did I let Marissa do it like this?"

Jules was mumbling to herself while she drove up the long, straight country road from Camden to the farmhouse. She'd been wondering that same thing for the last week or so as the final week of Parker's trial period came closer, along with her parents' anniversaries.

It was a lot – fielding emails and calls from the lawyer, who was trying to set up an appointment to sign the property title over to Parker... mentally steeling herself to get past the most difficult days of the year... and trying to figure out how much she should let Parker into the grieving process.

She was sweet – she always was – and she'd been doing a million little things all week to make Jules feel better. A pat of butter in the shape of a heart on her breakfast toast. An *I love you* note slipped into her wallet when Jules wasn't looking. A wildflower from the patch growing behind the barn threaded through her steering wheel when she went out to her truck. All the distracting, hot sex she could handle.

All of it helped – it made the week just a little easier to bear. But it also made the pain of the loss that much more acute, knowing she wasn't the only one who was thinking about it.

Today, she'd woken up feeling like her brain had been replaced with gelatin because on this day one year ago, her mother died of complications due to breast cancer. Parker had smothered her in hugs and kisses and made her a special breakfast of French toast and eggs to make sure she felt loved and supported, but that feeling in her head just didn't go away.

"You should stay home with me," Parker had said after Jules got out of the shower and started to dress in her scrubs, intending to go to the clinic like normal.

Jules managed a small smile at the fact that Parker had lately started to refer to the farmhouse as theirs. She hadn't even been inside her apartment in what felt like forever, and even though she could hardly think today, it felt good to call this place home again – to call Parker home.

"Emmy Daniels is bringing her mastiff in for a nail trim today," Jules had answered. "That's a two-person job – Shawn can't handle it on his own."

"Emmy can help him," Parker said, wrapping her arms around Jules and pressing her face into the curve of her neck. "You work so hard – you deserve a personal day every now and then."

And today is the mother of all personal days, Jules filled in mentally, wryly adding to herself, *and Friday will be the father of all personal days.*

"I'd rather work," she said. "Keep my mind busy, you know?"

Parker nodded, trying to understand, and she let Jules go. Unfortunately, even Emmy's mastiff couldn't keep her mind occupied enough to stop her from crying in her office when Shawn made an off-hand comment about taking his kids to see their grandparents that weekend.

Nina was the one who finally forced her out the door around noon, saying, "Honey, you just need to go home and be with Parker right now. There's nothing at the clinic that can't wait until next week – I know you're my boss, but I'm twenty years your senior and I'm telling you to take a vacation. Shawn and I will hold down the fort."

Jules smiled and sniffed, wiping away an errant tear. "I should write you up for insubordination," she teased.

Nina snorted. "Okay, you do that first thing Monday morning."

And so Jules drove home, her mind feeling ever so slightly less gelatinous, thinking about all the things she had to juggle this week and looking forward to crawling into bed with Parker and doing none of them today. Nina was right – she needed time, space.

What she found when she came into the kitchen was Parker up to her elbows in The Happy House Rabbit orders and Lucky hopping around her feet, hoping to capitalize on a dropped piece of banana or carrot.

"Oops," she said as she purposely nudged a little bit

of carrot off the counter. It rolled across the floor and Lucky hopped after it, and Parker looked up. "Hey, you're back early."

"Nina sent me home," Jules explained. "I cried in front of the mastiff."

"Aww, baby," Parker said, quickly wiping her hands and wrapping her arms around Jules. She kissed her cheeks, still a little bit puffy and warm from the tears, then the tip of her nose, her eyelids, and finally her lips. "Well, I'm glad you're here. Anything I can do to help?"

"Put me to work?" Jules suggested.

The orders that were coming in had slowed down a little once Parker's shop was no longer featured on the front page of Etsy – they were now at a manageable level – but she was still doing good business, enough to hire Shawn's daughter to help out for a couple of hours each weekend. Jules loved to see her confident and self-sufficient.

"You got a deal," Parker said, tossing Jules the apron that her dad always used when he grilled. It said *Don't just stand there – get me a beer,* and Jules laughed.

"Where did you find this?" she asked.

"It was on a hook in the pantry," Parker told her. "Should I have left it there?"

"No, it's fine," Jules said, putting it on. "My mom bought this for my dad as a gag gift the day he bought his charcoal grill. She didn't actually mean for him to wear it but I don't think he ever grilled without it."

"That's cute," Parker said. "My dad has one that says *Last time I cooked, hardly anyone got sick.*"

Jules snorted, then crossed the kitchen and pulled Parker into a fierce hug, kissing her deeply.

When she finally let her go, Parker asked, "What was that for?"

"I didn't think I'd have any reason to laugh today," she said. "So thank you."

They worked on filling treat orders for the next hour and a half, occasionally dropping tasty crumbs on the floor for Lucky and he'd run so fast to gobble them up that his paws spun out on the slick tile.

Then when all the treats were in the oven and their aprons were folded over the back of the kitchen chair, Parker took Jules' hand. "Come with me – I've got something for you."

"Oh yeah?" Jules asked, giving her an exaggeratedly sexy look even though she wasn't quite sure she was up for that today.

Parker just shook her head at her and led Jules into the living room. They sat down on the couch and Parker slid a white cardboard box about the size of a ream of paper across the coffee table to her.

As Jules brought it closer to her, feeling the weight of whatever was inside, Parker said, "I wanted to make something for you to remember them by, maybe to look through whenever you're missing them."

Jules could feel her chest tightening before she'd even opened the box. She lifted the lid and found a neatly bound, faux leather scrapbook. "Parker..." she breathed, lifting it out of the box. The emotions were choking her already and Parker scooted closer, looping her arms around Jules' waist and resting her cheek against her shoulder.

"You don't have to look through it in front of me if you don't want," she said as Jules opened the book and saw her parents' wedding portrait.

Her mom was in a quintessentially eighties gown – all lace and big sleeves – and her dad still had all his hair... a bit too much of it, in keeping with the fashion at the time. Jules laughed again. "Did you know my dad was Tom Selleck?"

Parker laughed. "That *is* a pretty epic moustache."

Jules flipped slowly through the pages. Parker had carefully arranged the photos chronologically – from newlyweds to homeowners, fawning over their first rabbit, a little spotted lop named Harvey, and then into her mom's pregnancy and at last, the appearance of baby Jules.

"You had quite a lot of hair yourself," Parker teased when they got to her newborn photo, a brand-new baby with a full head of hair.

"Yeah, I took after my dad," Jules agreed. "No moustache, thank God."

There were pictures of her mom holding a bunny in one arm and toddler Jules in the other, and pictures of Jules learning to ride a bike with her dad holding the handlebars. There were newspaper clippings from when they first established the rescue, and others later on celebrating the good work they were doing in the community.

Jules was openly crying by the time she got to the end of the book, where prayer cards for both of her parents were neatly fastened to the last page. She used the bottom of her shirt to wipe away the tears, trying not to waterlog the scrapbook, and when she set it down on the table, Parker scooped her into her arms.

"I'm sorry," she said, kissing the top of Jules' head and tucking it under her chin. "I didn't want to make you cry. I just thought—"

"No, it's a good cry," Jules said, letting the tears flow freely. She just cried against Parker's chest for at least five minutes, and Parker stroked her hair before letting her go. It was like a dam breaking inside of her, and by the time she sat up again, it *looked* like a dam had broken on the front of Parker's shirt. "Sorry," she said, dabbing at the wet spot.

"It's okay," Parker said. "Sometimes you just have to let it out."

"I haven't really let it out since they died," Jules confessed. "I cried a little at the funerals, but I didn't want the whole town to see me lose my shit so I held it in as best I could. And ever since then, I just kept holding it in because after a while, it felt too dangerous to let it out. I thought if I ever started crying, I'd never stop."

But she had. She'd cried and Parker had been there to hold her, and the release felt good.

"Do you feel any better now?" Parker asked gently.

Jules nodded. "A lot, actually. Parker, you are incredible and I can't believe you made this for me."

She picked up the scrapbook, flipping through the middle section again – the photos that depicted her as an awkward tween and then a somewhat gangly teen, with rabbits in nearly every one of the shots.

"I'd do anything for you," Parker said. "I love you."

"I love you too... so much," Jules said. "I haven't seen those pictures in years. Where did you find them?"

"There were some dusty photo albums in a cabinet in the dining room," Parker said. "I figured nobody had looked at them for years so it would be okay to steal a few pictures out of them. The rest I found in an old archival box in the attic."

Jules hugged the scrapbook to her chest. "This is the best gift I've ever received. Thank you."

Parker kissed her, and then the oven timer went off. She got up, letting her hand linger on Jules' shoulder as long as she could before she had to step away and tend to the treats.

Jules followed her into the kitchen, coming up behind Parker just as she was laying a cookie sheet full of finished treats on the counter. She wrapped her arms around her waist, relishing the sensation of Parker's curves against her body, and said, "I am so thankful for you. When I came up with the idea for that contest, I was just desperate to solve a problem, but when you showed up and I saw how good you were with the rabbits, I felt like I'd hit the jackpot. You were exactly who I was looking for to take over the rescue, and believe me, it didn't take long to realize you were the one I've been looking for my whole life, too. You're my other half, Parker."

She turned in Jules' arms, moisture making her eyes

shiny, and Jules laughed as she swiped it away with the pad of her thumb.

"Don't you start crying too," she said. "We'll have to build a boat soon if we don't stop."

Parker smiled, but there was something a little guarded in the way she looked at Jules, then turned her face away to dab at the tears forming in the corner of her eyes. It only lasted an instant – Jules was half-convinced she'd imagined it – and when Parker looked back at her, she was giving her a real smile this time. "You're my other half, too. I can't even imagine my life without you anymore."

It wasn't until almost a week later, on Monday morning, that Jules finally found out what the guarded look in Parker's eyes had been all about.

They'd made it through the rest of the week relatively unscathed and dry-eyed, and Jules had forgotten all about that moment of hesitation in the kitchen. It had been a hell of a hard week, but Parker was the one and only person Jules wanted to spend it with and as she was getting ready to go back to work, she made a mental note to thank Nina for telling her – nay, demanding for her – to take the rest of the week off.

She came downstairs in her scrubs and found Parker sitting at the kitchen table, a cup of coffee in her hands as she stared out the window at the barn.

Jules grabbed a cup of her own, asking, "Hey, babe, something wrong?"

"No," Parker said, but her words weren't exactly spoken with conviction.

There was a definite cloud cast over Parker's expression, and a momentary panic rose in Jules' chest. Today was the day she would sign the property over to Parker – they had an appointment at two with Marissa to make it all official. Was Parker second-guessing things, questioning whether she wanted to be legally tied to this place?

There was nothing about her demeanor or her actions over the last three months that would lead Jules to believe that, but the fear ripped through her nonetheless. Something was wrong – she could feel it.

"Actually," Parker said abruptly, "can you sit down for a minute? There's something I need to tell you."

Jules did, her heart hammering in her chest. She set down her own coffee cup and proceeded to let the liquid grow cold just like Parker's. She folded her hands between her knees and leaned toward her girlfriend, wondering what the hell was about to come at her.

"What's wrong?" she asked.

Parker let out a long sigh and said, "I never entered your contest."

Jules furrowed her brows. "What? How's that possible?"

"You know my friend, Kani?" Parker said, her face turning red as she pushed through the confession. Jules nodded. "Well, sometimes she can overstep her bounds a bit when she thinks she's helping. She knew about the contest and she knew I loved the idea, but David never would have gone for it – his whole life was in Chicago. And when we broke up and I moved home, I thought the best thing was to stick close to my parents. I was afraid to make another big change so soon after the first one. My treat business was barely getting a trickle of orders, and I felt totally off-balance. I didn't think I had it in me back then to run a rabbit rescue."

"I don't understand," Jules said. "You responded when I emailed you about your submission."

"Kani submitted the essay in my name," Parker said. "She put down my email address and I didn't know a thing about it until I got your email."

Jules narrowed her eyes. "But you didn't tell me that when I contacted you?"

Parker's eyes fell, staring into her lukewarm coffee. "That's because I wanted it. I was shocked and confused, but Kani told me what she'd done and convinced me to play along. Even though I didn't enter the contest, this place is my dream – you know that, Jules."

"And you didn't tell me at any point in the last twelve weeks," Jules said, anger replacing the anxiety that had been filling her chest. "Parker, you had so many opportunities to tell me the truth."

"I know," she said. "Believe me, I wanted to. I was going to tell you so many times but Kani—"

"Kani," Jules said, cutting her off. "What, so you let David run your life for twelve years and then when you finally put your foot down, you just let Kani take over?"

It was mean and she regretted it the moment the words came out of her mouth, but that was the thing about words – they couldn't be pulled back in. Parker looked her in the eyes and Jules saw hurt there, a hurt that matched her own pain at having been lied to for the last three months.

She sighed. "Why tell me now?"

"I couldn't let you sign your parents' property over to me without telling you the truth," Parker said. "I'll understand if you want to cancel the meeting this afternoon."

Jules looked at the clock hanging on the wall. It was a couple minutes to nine and she had to meet John McCade at his farm to do a wellness check on the two new kids in fifteen minutes. She'd barely make it there on time if she left right now.

She stood up. "I don't really know how I feel right now, other than deceived. I wish you'd just told me right away – it should have been the first thing out of your mouth when you got here."

"I was scared," Parker said. "I was sure if you heard that my contest entry was a lie, you'd send me packing and pick someone else. Don't tell me you wouldn't have done that if your first impression of me was that I was a liar."

Jules thought about it. Parker was probably right, but was it any better to know now after three months together, after falling in love, that she was a liar?

"I have to go to work," she said, picking up her untouched coffee cup. "I need to think about all this – I'll call you."

"Okay," Parker said meekly.

Jules dumped her cold coffee in the sink, then gave Parker a somewhat cursory kiss and an *I love you* before she left. While she drove out to the McCade farm, she ran the conversation back through her mind a few times and the whole thing left a bitter taste in her mouth – not just what Parker had done, but how Jules had responded.

It hurt, sure, but she'd come clean in the end.

Jules had no idea how to respond, and no one to confide in. *It would be great to have a mom to talk to right about now...*

16
PARKER

Parker sat at the kitchen table for a while after Jules left, staring into her coffee cup. She replayed their conversation in her head, trying to figure out just how upset Jules had been about the lie.

She was absolutely right – Parker should have told her right away, and she'd wanted to. But she was afraid, first because she was falling for the rabbits, and then because she was falling for Jules. She didn't want to lose her.

When Jules left for work, she'd kissed Parker, said she loved her, but were they empty gestures?

A little lump was forming in the back of Parker's throat and she couldn't help thinking about all the times when David used to say he loved her, without any real conviction in his voice, like his mind was elsewhere – on his career, his own troubles and concerns.

Jules is not David, she reminded herself, swallowing hard. *She wouldn't say something she didn't mean.*

It was at least half an hour later than usual by the time Parker finally got motivated to get up from the table and begin her morning chores. First, she took a minute to send Kani a message.

I told Jules about the essay. She's angry and says I should have told her sooner.

It was all she could do not to add, *I told you so,* but what would that accomplish? She couldn't afford to have her best friend upset with her too. It was about four-thirty in the afternoon in Helsinki, but Kani must have been busy, studying maybe, or talking to Phillies girl, because she didn't answer right away.

Parker checked her Etsy shop – ten more orders waiting in her queue – and then the Wakefield Rabbit Rescue Facebook page. There was a message waiting in her inbox.

Hi, I was wondering if the little white bunny, Cotton, is still available? She's so cute!
  Rachel Henson

Parker smiled. Poor Cotton had been waiting for her fur-ever home since before Parker got here and it was entirely possible that Rachel Henson would come to the same conclusion that a lot of other potential adopters had, that Cotton was too rambunctious, too destructive… but at least it was a nibble.

Hi Rachel,
  Yes, Cotton's still here and she'd love to meet you.

Let me know what day and time works best for you to come by and see her.
 – Parker

She sent her reply, feeling a little twisted up in her belly. Jules had said she needed to think about her lie. That would almost definitely take longer than a day, and she couldn't imagine them signing the title paperwork this afternoon. Who knew if Jules would want her here at all when she was finished thinking? Maybe Parker would be gone by the time Rachel wrote back and Jules would have to take over the rescue again.

All those thoughts vied for room in her head, fighting each other while she tried to remain calm, keep from expecting the worst. She went outside to clean the rabbit stalls and give the bunnies their breakfast, putting on the old galoshes that she knew had belonged to Jules' mother.

As she worked, she realized that she didn't need anyone else to help her pursue her dreams... but she wanted Jules to be part of her future. She wanted that more than anything. She announced to the rabbits, "I'm going to fix this. I'll do whatever it takes to make it right because I love her."

She drew in a deep breath, slowly exhaling, then she grabbed a rake and headed into the first stall in the row to start her morning chores. When she got to Cotton's stall, she crouched down and petted the little white rabbit that reminded her so much of her childhood bunny, Snowball.

"Guess what, girl?" she said. "There's a nice lady named Rachel who wants to meet you, but you gotta work with me. No biting, no destroying the living room, no sexy times with Lucky while she's visiting. Best behavior because she could be your fur-ever mommy."

She sighed as she stood up and started raking out the old hay to be replaced with fresh stuff. Jules was her forever – Parker just had to make things right.

17

JULES

Jules was still ruminating on what Parker had told her by the time she got into Camden, and she was also working on a headache due to caffeine withdrawal.

She stopped at Norie's Place on her way to the clinic to fix the easier of her two problems. The café was busy as it always was in the mornings – Hannah did a great business with the coffee-drinking crowd – and while Jules stood in line, she texted Shawn and Nina to ask if they wanted anything.

Then she opened her last text thread with Parker.

They'd gotten into the habit of messaging each other throughout the day. Parker would send Jules pictures and videos when the bunnies did cute things. Jules would sneak into her office and pull up her scrub top, giving Parker a little preview of what she had in mind for their evening. Or sometimes they'd just play a game they'd invented where they sent each other strings of meaningless emojis and made the other tell a story out of it.

The last text Jules had sent to Parker was a mermaid, a middle finger and a peacock. She'd just scrolled through her emojis and jabbed randomly to arrive at those ones, and Parker had written back, *Obviously it's Ariel giving the middle finger to life 'unda da sea' AND the handsome prince and going off to start her new life as a fabulous, sassy peacock.*

Jules had laughed out loud at that and Shawn had given her a weird look for it, and it made her smile now too. There was no denying that Parker had made her life better – lighter – and the unique way that she looked at the world was one of Jules' favorite things about her.

She loved Parker.

She wanted to be with her.

But she wasn't quite ready to forgive her for that lie. It wasn't something that could just be swept under the rug – because Jules was hurt, and also because it had occurred to her on her drive back from the McCade farm that it could cause problems with the contest.

"Whoa, somebody looks cranky," Hannah said, drawing Jules' attention up from her phone. She found that she was next in line, and maybe it was that crankiness that had kept the people behind her from nudging her forward.

"Sorry," she muttered to them, stepping up to the counter. "Can I get a large coffee, whatever you have brewed that's the strongest?"

She looked back down at her phone and found a

message from Nina – *Nothing for me hon, but Shawn says he'd love a mocha latte.*

"And a mocha latte," she added to Hannah. "To go."

"Hello to you too," Hannah said, punching the order into her cash register. "Get up on the wrong side of the bed today?"

"Sorry," Jules muttered, for the second time in under a minute. "Parker and I got in a fight and I haven't had my coffee yet."

"Oh no," Hannah said. "Everything okay?"

Jules let out a long sigh while Hannah moved down the counter and started making the drinks. "I don't know. We were supposed to meet with the estate lawyer this afternoon to sign the property title over to Parker, did you know that?"

Hannah shook her head. They never did have that double date that she'd been wanting – time flew way too fast – but Jules and Parker came to the café often and sometimes Hannah had time to sit down with them for a few minutes and chat. Sometimes Avery joined them too, and they'd talk about life, the rescue, love... everything that was going on in their lives. Jules had known Hannah and Avery for years, but now the four of them were getting to be good friends.

"Well, this morning out of nowhere, Parker tells me that her contest entry was a sham," Jules said, trying to keep her voice low but ending up having to shout over the sound of Hannah frothing milk for the latte. "She never even entered – her friend wrote her essay, and Parker never said anything to me."

"Oh wow," Hannah said. "And you're mad that she lied to you?"

"Yes... no... I don't know what to think," Jules said. "I wish she'd told me sooner, but if she had, maybe we never would have had time to get to know each other and fall in love. What I think I'm the most worried about is the contest terms – if her entry was forged, is she even eligible to 'win' the property? That could mean big legal trouble if the other applicants found out."

"Oh fudge," Hannah said. "I didn't even think of that."

"It could turn into some big scandal in the news," Jules said, gratefully taking the black coffee that Hannah passed across the counter to her and taking a long sip. "My contest went viral in a minor way, and now Parker's treat business is going viral in a bigger way, and if people find out that I signed the property over to someone who didn't enter the contest *and* is now my girlfriend... it could ruin both of our reputations. I just don't know what to do."

"You'll figure it out," Hannah said, passing the mocha to her too. "Sounds like you need to talk to that estate lawyer and get some advice."

"Yeah, you're probably right," Jules said. "Thanks – for listening and for the coffee."

"You're welcome," Hannah said. Before Jules had time to say anything else, she was already back at the other end of the counter, helping the long line of customers waiting for her.

Jules headed outside, walking up the block to where

she'd parked her truck on the street, but before she was even halfway there, someone was calling out behind her.

"Excuse me, Jules Wakefield?"

She turned, confused at first, and saw a man in a suit jogging toward her, a cup of Norie's Place coffee in one hand. As he got closer, she realized he looked familiar, but she couldn't place him just yet.

"Yes?"

"Justin Manning," he said, holding his hand out to her. The name snapped everything into place – the developer who wanted to knock down her parents' house. She took his hand reluctantly as he said, "I'm with Manning and Manning Realty. We spoke last fall"

"Oh yeah," she said. "I remember."

She thought she'd been pretty clear about her feelings on Manning's plans a year ago – over her dead body – and the coffee she'd gotten into her system was delicious but it hadn't reached critical mass yet and she still had a raging headache. It was all she could do not to snap, *what do you want?*

"I hope you can forgive me, but I happened to overhear what you were saying back there, to the café owner," Manning said. Jules shot daggers at him with her eyes and he added, "I wasn't listening on purpose. I just happened to be sitting nearby."

"Okay…" she said. She had way too much shit going on today and this man was truly testing her patience.

"I'm still interested, you know," he said.

"Well, I'm not," Jules told him, turning to go.

"I'll pay you more than market value," he said to her back, and when she kept walking, he called, "Double."

That got her to turn back around. She could practically see the relief on his face. She walked back to him and asked, "Why are you so hell-bent on buying my parents' property? Why is it that valuable to you?"

"Camden is an emerging market," he said. "The population has nearly doubled in the last fifteen years and the local economy is doing better than it ever has. My partner and I see great potential in getting in on the ground floor of a budding city like this and your property is optimally located for a new residential neighborhood."

"I told you before that I have no intention of selling to you," she said, "unless you want to run a rabbit rescue, that is."

"Again, forgive me for overhearing, but it sounds like that's not working out so well for you," Manning said.

His tone was that of the quintessential smarmy businessman and it actually made Jules' lip curl involuntarily as he kept on talking, oblivious to her distaste.

"What's better?" he asked. "Selling your property at a profit and relocating your little bleeding-heart rabbit rescue literally anywhere you want with all that money – you could rescue rabbits in Jamaica if you wanted to – or sticking it out where you are and getting hit with legal action for running a dishonest contest with a prize that you were always planning to give to your girlfriend?"

Jules' blood ran cold. A few minutes ago she'd been worried about other contest entrants and how they might react if they found out about Parker's lie. Now she was staring into this real estate developer's cold, stony eyes and wondering if he was actually threatening to blackmail her with that information.

"That's not what happened. Stay out of it," she said through clenched teeth, then turned and walked away – more determined this time.

That tiny little threat would do nothing if Justin Manning had already made up his mind to sink his claws into her property, but it was the best she could muster in the moment. She just had to get away from him, get some more coffee into her system, and then she could figure out what the hell to do.

Just as she was climbing into her truck, she heard Manning call to her one more time. She tried to ignore him, but the words reached her anyway. "That offer has an expiration date, Jules. Double the market value and your problems melt away, but you gotta give me an answer by the end of the day."

Or what, the blackmailing begins in earnest? she wondered, but she didn't have the stomach to talk back to him. She slammed her truck door and took a deep, steadying breath, then picked up her phone to tell Shawn he wasn't getting his mocha latte after all. She needed to go home to Parker and come up with a plan – together.

She was halfway through a text when the phone started ringing in her hand. *Wakefield Veterinary Clinic* – the office's main number. Jules picked it up. "Nina?"

"Are you on your way?" she asked. "The Andersons' new puppy ate a bee and had a severe allergic reaction – he's having trouble breathing."

"Shit," Jules said. "Have Shawn administer epinephrine and I'll be right there – I'm just around the corner."

So much for going home to Parker... Jules gave a cursory look behind her then peeled out into the street, probably making Justin Manning – who was still standing on the sidewalk – wonder what the hell her problem was.

18

PARKER

It was close to eleven before Parker finally got through all her morning chores and went inside to whip up a couple quick batches of treats to fulfill the day's orders. She worked as fast as she could, with her eye on the prize – going into town and catching Jules at the clinic, finding a way to make things up to her – but the faster she worked, the more endless her stack of orders felt.

Talk about a mixed blessing, she thought as she pressed raw treat mix into silicone molds again and again. She was grateful for all the new customers she was acquiring, but right at this moment, she longed for the days when she'd log in and find not a single order had come in overnight.

She just wanted to get to Jules, to plead with her to understand why she'd lied.

At least Kani was around to keep her mind occupied.

By the time Parker got back from the barn, there was a message waiting for her on Bunny Central.

KaniConeja: Voi paska... shit. I'm sorry Parks. Here if you need to talk.

Parker set up her laptop on the kitchen counter and Skyped Kani while she made treats.

"I guess I should have let you go with your gut," Kani said as soon as the call connected. "Is she still mad?"

"I don't know," Parker told her. "She had to go to work."

"So... what are you going to do about the essay?" Kani asked as Parker put a baking sheet of treats in the oven. "About Jules?"

"I'm not going down without a fight," Parker told her.

"Good," Kani said. "And if you think it'll help, I'm more than happy to talk to her – I'll tell her it was all my idea and that I'm a colossal busybody who can't keep her nose out of other people's business."

Parker laughed again. "Can I get that in writing?"

Finally, a little before one o'clock, all the treats were cooling on the counter and Parker gathered a bunch of wildflowers from behind the barn, then hopped in her car. She drove into town and parked in front of the clinic, her heart hammering in her chest by the time she got inside.

Nina looked up from her desk and smiled when she saw the flowers. "Looking for Jules?"

"Yeah," Parker said. "Is she busy?"

"She's in her office. Go on back."

Parker thanked her and walked down the short hallway behind the reception desk, glancing into the exam room where she and Jules had fixed Lucky up. Emotion swelled in her chest and tears threatened to spill onto her cheeks – what if Jules was so mad she couldn't forgive her? What if she'd ruined everything with one stupid mistake?

She found Jules hunched over her desk, scribbling patient notes in a chart and paying no attention when Parker stopped in the open doorway. She knocked softly. She gave Jules an apologetic little smile and said, "Hey."

Jules stood up, immediately forgetting her work. "What are you doing here?"

"I couldn't wait until you got off work," Parker said. "I wanted to tell you that I'm sorry. I never meant to deceive you and I'll do whatever it takes to make you believe that... help you trust me again."

Jules came around her desk and Parker held out the flowers – a peace offering that maybe was a little slapdash, but she'd just wanted to get to Jules as fast as she could. She didn't want to waste time going farther into town and trying to buy her nicer flowers, or something altogether better. She just wanted to see her, touch her, love her.

In any case, Jules ignored the flowers entirely. She pulled Parker into her office and elbowed the door shut.

She clicked the lock and pulled Parker into her arms in one smooth motion.

"It's okay," she murmured against Parker's lips, kissing her urgently and enfolding Parker in her arms. "It's okay, I understand. I love you."

"I love you too," Parker said, breathless and surprised. She surrendered to the kiss though, dropping the flowers on Jules' desk and threading her fingers through her hair. "I love you so much."

Jules had her pressed against the wall, their bodies colliding, hands groping at each other. She kept whispering against Parker's lips, in between kisses. "I wanted to come back and talk it out as soon as I stormed out. I'm glad you're here."

"Me too," Parker said. She had to break away after a moment, had to be sure. She cupped Jules' face in her hands, looking into her eyes as she asked, "Do you forgive me?"

Jules nodded. "You were right – if you'd told me right away, I never would have given you a chance. I'd have picked someone else, and that would have been the biggest mistake of my life because then I never would have fallen in love with you."

They kissed again, their tongues entwining and their hips straining toward each other, but then Jules broke away. "Parker, sit down. I have to tell you something."

Parker frowned, and didn't actually take a seat. Jules' entire demeanor had shifted in an instant and it made her stomach do a little flip. "What's wrong?"

"Remember when I told you about that real estate

developer that wanted to turn my parents' property into a housing development?" she asked.

Parker nodded – she was grateful that Jules never had to entertain that possibility.

"I stopped at Norie's Place for coffee on my way to the clinic this morning," Jules said. "I was upset and Hannah could see it. She asked me what was wrong and I told her about the essay. Of course it's just my luck that the only friggin' person in the world who shouldn't have overheard that conversation just so happened to be getting a coffee there too."

"The developer?" Parker asked, her brows knit. "I don't understand."

"He followed me outside, threatened me," Jules said.

"The bastard," Parker growled, clinging tighter to Jules, who sighed.

"The problem is he's not entirely off-base," Jules continued. "I created a contest and I can't legally give you the prize if you never entered, or if Kani entered you under false pretenses. He basically threatened to bring legal action against me if I didn't sell the property to him."

"Can he do that?" Parker asked, her chest tightening. This was all her fault... no matter what Jules said, no matter whether she forgave her, Parker knew in her heart that she should have confessed as soon as she figured out what Kani had done. And now... "You could lose the rescue, the house?"

Everything.

"I won't let him take it," Jules said. "I'll never let him

knock down my parents' house, dismantle the rescue. But we might have to give it up – pick a new contest winner, someone who actually submitted their own entry."

"I'm so sorry, Jules," Parker said. Her heart was breaking – for the rabbits she'd grown to love, for the house that felt like home but only when Jules was in it with her, and for everything she'd cost her because of one stupid lie.

"It's not your fault," Jules said, pulling her into a hug. "Honestly, babe, I'm *glad* you lied to me because it brought us together. Maybe it was always meant to be this way. Maybe there's something else for us."

Us...

Parker drew back, determination in her eyes. "There's got to be something we can do. I'm not going to stand idly by and let that soulless developer take it from you. I'll use my treat money to hire a lawyer. I'll pay whatever fines they come up with – we're not letting them take your house."

"He's been salivating over that land ever since my parents died," Jules said. "He's a vulture and he's got a hell of a lot more legal firepower than we'll ever be able to muster. I think the best we can do is pick a new contest winner – make sure the rescue goes to someone who'll run it well... although I can't imagine anyone who'll do a better job than you. Sometimes I think you care more about those bunnies than my parents did."

"I care about you," Parker said. "And us. And we'll figure this out."

Jules rested her head on Parker's shoulder, wrapping her arms around her waist. "I'm glad you're here."

"Me too," Parker said. "I'm sorry you had to talk to that asshole all by yourself."

"It's my fault for not just talking it out with you right away," Jules said. "The kids could wait."

Parker kissed her forehead, asking, "How are they?"

Jules smiled. "They're good. Freaking adorable. I've got pictures."

She fished out her phone and showed them to Parker, and then Parker said, "Oh, guess what?"

"What?"

"Somebody messaged me on Facebook about Cotton," she told Jules. "Her name's Rachel and she seems nice – maybe *somebody's* going to get a happy ever after today."

Jules lifted her head. "As long as I have you, I have everything I need. If you promise me you're not going anywhere, then I know I can get through anything Justin Manning or anyone else throws at me."

"Of course I'm not going anywhere," Parker said. "I love you. Forever."

"Forever," Jules said.

"What time is it?" Parker wondered aloud, reaching for her phone. "If we haven't missed the appointment, maybe your estate lawyer can refer us to whatever type of lawyer we need to combat the real estate developer."

"It's one forty-five," Jules said, taking out her phone. "We can make it if we leave now."

19

JULES

Marissa's office was on the other side of Camden, although to call it an office was being generous. It was a very nicely appointed, roomy outbuilding behind the lawyer's house – a converted shed that now sported travertine tile floors and plush velvet couches full of throw pillows.

A lot of the entrepreneurs around Camden ran their businesses like that – out of their homes – although the winds had been changing along with all the development and growth that the little town was going through.

"Come on in," Marissa said when she spotted Jules and Parker coming up the stone walkway. "You're right on time." And, when she noticed they were both breathing a little heavier than usual, she added, "Gosh, what did you do, jog here?"

"We were running a little late," Jules explained as Marissa pointed them to the couch and pulled a couple chilled bottles of water out of a mini-fridge under her desk. "We've got a bit of a problem with the contest."

That was understating it, but they'd get into the details soon enough.

Marissa handed them each a bottled water and Parker said, "Thanks."

Then Marissa leaned against the front of her desk, hands curled around the edge, and asked, "What kind of problem? Are you thinking of backing out, Parker?"

"Not by choice," she said, and Marissa furrowed her brows. Parker added, "I'm afraid I made kind of a mess of things."

"Okay," Marissa said, going around her desk and sitting down, adopting a more serious posture. She pointed to a small stack of about twenty legal-sized papers, saying, "I figured today's appointment would just be signing paperwork – I've got it all drawn up here – but it sounds like you better fill me in instead. What's going on?"

Jules told her everything – the application Kani completed in Parker's name, the offer that Justin Manning had made nine months ago and the veiled threat he'd made this morning, and her decision along with Parker that they'd sooner select a new contest winner than give in to Manning's blackmail.

By the time she finished, she was feeling a little bit sick to her stomach and wondering why she thought an essay contest in exchange for a piece of real estate was ever a good idea. Parker took her hand, and it made her feel just a little bit better.

But Marissa just leaned back in her chair. "Is that everything?"

"Yes. So, what are our options?"

Marissa just shrugged. "Cancel the contest. Simple."

"Cancel it?" Jules asked, shooting a confused look at Parker.

"I know how much you wanted to get the property off your hands, Jules," Marissa said. "But you're just going to have to hold onto it a bit longer." She looked at Parker, at the way Jules' hand was enveloped in hers on Parker's lap, and added, "I have an inkling your feelings on that have changed over the last few months anyway."

That was true – before Parker moved in, Jules couldn't imagine a set of events that would bring her back into that house, feeling comfortable there and not like her parents' ghosts were tugging at her heartstrings every minute she was inside her childhood home. Now, she slept there every night with Parker curled up against her side, and it was beginning to feel like home again.

But...

"How can I just cancel the contest?" she asked. "Doesn't that breach the contract terms just the same as awarding a winner who never entered it?"

Marissa smiled and sat up a little taller in her leather executive chair. "What do you take me for, a shyster? I included a clause in the contract giving you the right to back out at any time, for any reason, to protect your interests – just like the three-month trial period was intended to do."

Jules felt a weight lift from her chest. "So that's it? Just say the contest is over, there was no winner?"

"Yep," Marissa said. "You won't be able to sign the property over to Parker today – that'd look a bit too convenient and give your real estate developer friend too much ammo – but if you can maintain your current arrangement for, let's say a year, we can sign the papers then."

Jules relaxed backward into the couch, nearly being swallowed up by all the throw pillows. She exhaled a long sigh of relief and looked at Parker. "That work for you?"

"Of course," Parker said. "I don't care about owning the property – I never really did. I just want to rescue bunnies and be with you."

She leaned back and gave Jules a quick kiss, and Marissa was noisily stacking the title paperwork, tapping it on her desk to remind the two of them that she was still in the room – that they were, in fact, in her office. Jules sat back up and Marissa dropped the whole stack of papers into a heavy-duty shredder beside her desk. While it made confetti out of them, Marissa said sternly, "You know what would have helped you bypass this whole problem, though?"

"What?" Jules asked.

"Actually *reading* the contract when I gave it to you six months ago," she said, miffed. "You would have known about the cancellation clause and you could have thrown it in Manning's face as soon as he threatened you. I *knew* you were lying when you told me you read it."

"I'm sorry," Jules said. "I really did mean to, but it was just too much at the time. I still hadn't really cried over my parents and I was bottling a lot up. But things are better now."

She took Parker's hand again, kissing her knuckles, and Marissa snorted. "All right, love bunnies – get out of my office before you make me nauseous. If Manning contacts you again, have him give me a call and I'll set him straight."

"Thank you," Jules said, standing and shaking Marissa's hand across the expansive desk.

Then she opened the door, holding it for Parker, and as soon as they were outside, she bent down and wrapped her arms around Parker's waist, lifting her up and spinning her around. Parker laughed, and when her feet were on solid ground again, she kept her arms around Jules' shoulders and asked, "Are you happy?"

"Never been happier," Jules said. "I love you, Parker."

"I love you too," she answered. "Do you have to go back to work?"

Jules shook her head. "Not right now. Let's go home."

They barely made it into the house before Jules caught Parker in her arms again. Lucky stood on his hind feet in his pen in the corner of the living room, wanting to get in on the loving as Jules embraced Parker.

"Hey," she said. "Thank you."

"What for?"

"For being exactly who I was looking for when I created that contest," she said. "And for being exactly what I needed too, even though I had no idea."

Parker laughed. "Well, I guess we should thank Kani for playing our unwitting matchmaker. You don't hate her for falsifying my entry, do you?"

"How could I?" Jules asked. "Without her, I wouldn't have you. I never would have found my forever."

She kissed Parker, love turning quickly to passion on their lips, and walked her backward across the living room until Parker's heels bumped against the couch.

They were shedding layers of clothing quickly, stripping each other's shirts off and touching, kissing, licking at the skin that was exposed along the way. Jules dropped down to her knees, running her tongue lightly along the soft line down the center of Parker's stomach and swirling teasingly around her belly button until she felt Parker's intake of breath suck her stomach inward.

Jules popped the button of Parker's jeans and looked up into her entrancing eyes as she yanked her pants downward. Parker nibbled her lower lip, running her hands through Jules' hair as she stepped out of her jeans. Then Jules nudged her thighs apart and brought her mouth to the soft mound before her, breathing Parker in and letting her own hot breath permeate the thin fabric of Parker's panties.

She shivered with the sensation, her hands going to the back of Jules' head and drawing her mouth more firmly against her. She let out a grunt as Jules' tongue found her clit through the fabric, letting her know how badly she wanted her, and Jules felt her own body responding in kind. Warmth and wetness rushed between her thighs and she had to have her.

Jules pulled Parker's panties down, revealing her sex already swollen with desire, and the sight alone had her own core throbbing with the need for relief.

She took Parker by the hands, tugging her downward to sit on the couch, and Jules knelt before her.

"You're so beautiful," she said, sliding one finger up and down through her slick folds. "You're perfect," she breathed. Then she bowed her head to taste her... and snapped her head back up when she heard a racket from Lucky's corner of the living room.

Parker was laughing, and Jules turned to see the little scamp sitting innocently on the outside of his pen, looking at them as if to say, *What? Nothing to see here.*

Jules turned back to Parker. "Looks like we have another Houdini on our hands. Should we catch him?"

Parker shook her head adamantly. "Leave him. I need you."

She reached down, tugging playfully on Jules' hair until she had no choice but to go along with it or be left behind and bald. She stood and Parker made quick work of her scrub pants and boxers, tossing them to the floor and then taking Jules' hips in her hands. She pulled Jules onto her lap, straddling her with her palms grasping her ass and squeezing.

Lucky was all but forgotten the moment Parker leaned forward and took Jules' nipple into her mouth, sucking and twirling around it with her tongue. The sensation released a flood of desire through Jules' body and she slid her hand into the tight space between them, her fingers finding the erect nub of Parker's clit.

"Mmm," she moaned as soon as Jules touched her, the vibration of her mouth against Jules' nipple sending a new wave of pleasure through her.

Parker put her hand between Jules' legs, playing through her slickness and pressing inside of her as she continued to tease her nipples. Jules closed her eyes, letting the sensations wash over her as she rubbed Parker's clit and enjoyed the way she moaned against her body.

She was getting closer to the edge with every touch, every lick. Heat was building in her core and she rocked her hips against Parker's hand—

And then a blur of brown fur streaked past her, up the couch cushion beside them and over the back of the couch before coming back down on the other side and racing across the floor. Parker and Jules froze, then dissolved into a fit of laughter as Lucky continued to zoom across the floor and demand to be part of the fun.

Jules leaned forward, draping herself over Parker and feeling her body continue to shake with laughter under her. "Do you think we should catch him now?"

"Nah, he's having fun," Parker said. "Such is life with bunnies. But I do think we should go upstairs for a bit."

"Good idea," Jules said, getting up and pulling Parker to her feet.

Lucky looked at them, wondering what he did to drive them away, and Parker retrieved one of her treats from a jar on a shelf above his pen to keep him busy for a little while. Then she tilted her head down, looking through her lashes at Jules as she hooked her finger at her.

"Come and get me," she said, walking backward toward the stairs.

Jules bit her lip, wasting no time following her.

On Saturday morning, Jules and Parker were sitting in the living room sipping their coffee and waiting for Rachel Henson to show up. Lucky had a houseguest in his indoor pen and Cotton was checking everything out as if she hadn't been in this room a couple dozen times already.

"Do you think she's plotting another escape?" Jules asked as they watched the little white cottontail explore.

"Probably," Jules said. "But if we're lucky – if Cotton is lucky – Rachel won't mind a mischievous bunny."

"They're the best kind," Parker said. "They keep you on your toes."

She was optimistic as always, forever hoping for the perfect match between bunny and adopter, but Jules knew Parker got a little nervous whenever it came to Cotton. She'd been here so long and she'd run off so many potential adopters with her impish behavior.

"Maybe we should just adopt her ourselves," Jules suggested. "If Rachel doesn't work out."

Parker pressed her lips together, then shook her head. "No, Rachel's gonna love her – I can feel it."

Rachel showed up about ten minutes later. She was in her mid-twenties and she had a warmth about her that Jules could feel immediately. She smiled easily and she positively melted when she saw Cotton and Lucky in the pen.

"Oh my gosh, is that her?" she asked, going over to the pen and dropping to her knees in front of Cotton. "She's even cuter than in the videos you posted."

"That's her all right," Parker said. "Would you like to play with her?"

Rachel's eyes lit up. "I'd love to."

Parker opened the pen – Cotton was at least polite enough to wait instead of finding an escape route of her own – and the two bunnies bounded out, running around the living room.

"Coffee?" Jules offered, but Rachel declined. She watched the rabbits with rapt adoration and after they'd had a chance to stretch their legs, they both came over and started sniffing at her, checking her out.

"Here, give her a treat and she'll love you forever," Parker said, taking a couple of Happy House Rabbit treats from the jar. She gave one to Rachel and fed the other to Lucky.

"Here you go, girl," Rachel said, and before she'd even had the chance to hand Cotton the treat, the little white rabbit was in her lap, paws on her chest and begging.

Parker turned to Jules with a sly smile, mouthing the words *I taught her that*. Jules tried not to laugh and she watched as Rachel fed Cotton, looking like she was about to explode from all the cuteness.

Cotton hopped down after a little while, doing some more exploring, and the three of them talked. It turned out that Rachel was an electrician and she was working on the Amazon Fulfillment Center building, but she'd fallen in love with Camden right away and she'd just bought her first house here, planning to stay after the job was done.

Parker told her all about Cotton, playing up her cuter and more lovable traits but also informing Rachel of just how destructive she could be if she got bored and figured out how to escape her pen.

"I had a dog that ate my shoe once when I was a kid," Rachel said with a laugh. "Like, my *whole* shoe, so trust me – I know all about destructive pets and I've been researching rabbit toys and habitats ever since I saw your Facebook page. I'm looking forward to finding entertaining ways to keep her busy."

Jules watched Parker's expression change the longer they talked to Rachel – from one of cautious optimism to full-on excitement. At last, she asked, "So, do you want her?"

"Of course," Rachel said just as Cotton came over and sniffed at her hand, then ran her chin over Rachel's finger – scent-marking her as her property and really sealing the deal.

"It looks like she wants you too," Parker said. She turned to Jules, moisture in her eyes as she added, "At last, she's got her fur-ever family."

And I've got mine, Jules thought, her heart full in a way she never knew was possible before Parker.

EPILOGUE
PARKER – ONE YEAR LATER

Parker sipped her coffee, her knee pressed up against Jules' beneath the kitchen table. It was starting to get late in the morning and she knew there were a lot of treat orders waiting for her – Monday mornings were always her busiest times – but she wanted to linger in this moment a few minutes longer.

Since Jules officially moved back into the farmhouse six months ago, they'd fallen into a really comfortable, cozy morning routine that Parker really loved.

They'd wake up with the sun but wind up staying in bed for a while longer most days, getting tangled up in the blankets and each other. Eventually, though, the day would have to begin. There would be coffee and breakfast, and they'd let Lucky hop around their feet in the kitchen. Then Jules would head off to the vet clinic and whatever awaited her there, and Parker would go out to the barn to give the rescue rabbits their morning meal and start her own work for the day.

It was a set of tasks she'd already repeated at least two hundred times since she got here, but she couldn't fathom ever getting tired of it all. She loved every second of it.

"How many orders do you have today?" Jules asked as she finished off her coffee.

"Lots," Parker said. "Christmas is coming up and there are a lot of pet gift guides online that are featuring my shop. I need to fill orders and also start stocking up on inventory so I don't fall behind when the holiday shopping really takes off."

"Sounds like you've got your work cut out for you today," Jules said, standing and giving her a kiss on the forehead before she went over to the sink to rinse out her coffee mug. "Hey, why don't you get started now? I'll take care of the rabbits this morning."

Parker furrowed her brows. "It's Monday – you do know that, right?"

Jules helped her out sometimes on the weekends along with Shawn's daughter, but during the week she always had to leave for the clinic so Parker was on her own.

But today she shrugged and said, "Yeah, but I texted Nina while you were in the shower and she said we don't have any appointments scheduled for this morning. I'll go in later."

"Oh," Parker said. It was odd, but she really did have a massive amount of treats to bake today – she wasn't about to look a gift horse in the mouth. "Thanks, babe. I appreciate it."

"Anything for you," Jules said, coming up behind her

and wrapping her arms around Parker. She kissed her again, Parker turning her head this time to capture her lips, and then she slipped into the old pair of her mom's galoshes that had turned into a sort of good luck charm around the farmhouse.

They could have bought new ones, a pair for each of them even, but without ever verbalizing it, they both seemed to decide that those old galoshes were the only ones they needed.

Jules disappeared out the back door, where there was a thin layer of frost coating the yard, and Parker shivered as a gust of cold air came in from the covered patio. Then she got up and went to her laptop, which had found a more or less permanent home on the kitchen counter because of how often she needed it there. Lucky followed her, circling around her feet and already hoping for dropped ingredients while Parker logged into her Etsy shop and started to look over the details of the day's orders.

Treats... treats... Christmas sampler box... treats... and a birthday cake with a special instruction. Parker had recently started customizing them with a little banner on top of each cake saying 'Happy Birthday' and the name of the rabbit, but for this one, the client requested, *Can you print 'Will you marry me?' instead of 'Happy Birthday'?*

"Awww," Parker said aloud, and Lucky looked up at her, wondering what all the fuss was about. Some bunny-lover out there was actually using her treats to propose to their partner! She looked out the window toward the barn, wanting to tell Jules, but all Parker could see was a faint trail of boot prints in the grass.

It'd have to wait til Jules came back inside.

Parker made the banner on her laptop, then sent it to the printer on a cart in the corner and started working on orders. She was halfway through grating all the carrots she'd need when she heard the ding of a Skype call coming in.

Parker nudged her keyboard with one elbow, trying not to get carrot juice all over it, and accepted the call. "Hey, what's up, Kani?"

"Nothing," Kani said. "Just wanted to say hi." She caught sight of the massive pile of ingredients that Parker had stacked up on the kitchen table and said, "Whoa, lots of orders today?"

"Yeah," Parker said. "Oh! I got a proposal cake!"

"What? Jules proposed?" Kani's eyes bugged out and Parker hurried to correct her, her cheeks turning slightly pink at the misunderstanding.

"No, no, no," she said. "Somebody ordered a treat cake from me but they want to use it to propose."

She held up the piece of cardstock on which she'd printed the little *Will you marry me?* banner, and Kani let out a nearly identical, "Awww."

"I wonder if they'll send me a picture after the fact," Parker said, "so I can include it on my Etsy shop."

She had all sorts of pictures of happy fur-customers on her shop by now, and she'd started to cross-promote the rescue to get more attention on the fact that rabbits were in need of homes, not just in Camden but everywhere. So far, it seemed to be working – she'd found homes for almost a hundred rabbits in her first year at Wakefield Rabbit Rescue.

"I bet they will," Kani said.

Parker went back to grating carrots, chatting with Kani about their weekends – she and Jules had gone on a double date with Hannah and Avery to a bar in town that had just started hosting trivia nights, and Kani was making long-distance work remarkably well with Phillies girl.

"How's everything going with that?" Parker prodded.

"Good," Kani said. "She's not a bunny fanatic yet but I can see the potential. I'll bring her over to the dark side."

Parker thought she heard the back door open and she looked through the window again, still wanting to tell Jules about the proposal cake, but she wasn't there.

"Where'd ya go?" Kani asked and Parker stepped back into frame.

"Sorry," she said. "Jules stayed home to help with the rabbits while I make treats. I thought I heard her."

"She's really sweet," Kani said. "And thoughtful. You're a lucky woman."

"I know I am," Parker said, and at that word, she remembered Lucky hopping around her feet, begging for crumbs. She looked down, dropping a piece of carrot for him, and was surprised to see a little orange bunny snatching it up instead. "How'd you get in here?"

Parker bent down to pick it up, and saw two more rescue bunnies from the barn hopping around the kitchen. Each of them had a silk ribbon tied around its neck, and they were dealing with that fact with varying amounts of grace. The little orange bun complacently let her pick him up, while an all-black lop near the door stood on its back feet and tried to use its paws to shed the ribbon.

Parker inspected the one around the orange bunny's neck and found a little piece of cardstock threaded through it like a gift tag. In Jules' careful handwriting, it said, *I love you fur-ever, Parker.*

"Jules?" Parker called, a silly grin on her face. "What are you up to?" She heard Kani giggling from the laptop and she said, "Hey, give me a minute. Jules is playing a prank on me or something."

She set the orange bunny down and went over to the black one, untying the ribbon to free him of it before she read the note. This one said, *I can't wait to set a world record with you for longest first date ever.*

Parker laughed, then chased down a couple more rabbits and read their notes.

You're the best thing that ever happened to me.

The rabbits aren't the only ones around here who are better for having known you.

And finally... *Where's Lucky?*

Parker smiled, looking around. there were at least half a dozen rabbits in the kitchen now, as if by magic, and Lucky was no longer one of them. She looked under the table, then glanced into the patio, and finally made her way into the living room where Lucky was sitting in the middle of the floor, a tiny white satin pillow tied around his neck.

Parker's heart started beating faster and her legs felt like jelly as she crossed the room and scooped him into her arms. There was a pretty gold band inlaid with diamonds tied to the pillow, along with the sheet of paper she'd printed earlier asking *Will you marry me?*

Parker's heart skipped a beat.

"Jules?" she called out, and then she appeared from around the corner of the dining room wall. "What on earth are you up to?"

"You know," Jules said with a grin. She came over and untied the ring from the pillow, then left Parker holding Lucky as she sank down to one knee. "Parker Rose, will you make me the luckiest woman in the world and be my wife?"

"Oh my God," Parker squeaked. "Yes. Yes, of course. Get up here!"

Jules laughed and got to her feet, barely having a chance to slide the ring onto Parker's finger before Parker was pulling her into a hug, smothering her in kisses. Lucky was sandwiched between them, looking like he loved every minute of the attention.

"I love you, I love you, I love you," Parker said, punctuating each statement with a kiss. "I can't believe you did all this. That cake order...?"

"Mine," Jules said. "And I enlisted the rabbits' help

because no proposal to you would be complete without bunnies."

"You're incredible," Parker said.

"Did you say yes?!" Kani shouted from the laptop, and Parker burst out laughing.

"And her?" she asked Jules. "Did you tell her to distract me while you did all this?"

Jules laughed. "Nope, she pretty much insisted on being present as soon as I told her what I was doing. Said she'd get on a plane to the United States and interrupt us at the front door if I didn't include her. We should probably go tell her the good news."

Parker set Lucky down and he trailed them back to the kitchen. She admired the ring as they walked, watching all the little diamonds glimmering in the light.

"You said you'd let me watch," Kani objected to Jules when they were back in the frame and Parker was holding out the ring, a huge grin on her face.

"Sorry," Jules said. "I only have so much control over the bunnies and Lucky decided the proposal was happening in the living room."

"I forgive you," Kani said. "But I better be a bridesmaid!"

"Done," Parker said. "But you better buy your plane ticket in a hurry because the way I feel right now, I don't want to wait another day to make this woman my wife."

A NOTE FROM CARA

Hello!

Thank you so much for reading *Lucky in Love* – with everything that's going wrong in the world, sometimes all we need is a quick escape and a reminder that there *are* still things that are beautiful... like new love and the unconditional affection of a furry family member.

I hope you enjoyed the first book in my Fur-ever Romance series. Turn the page for a one-chapter sneak peek at book two, *Foxy Lady,* featuring wildlife rehabilitator Sydney.

With love,
Cara

- facebook.com/caramalonebooks
- twitter.com/caramalonebooks
- goodreads.com/caramalonebooks
- bookbub.com/authors/cara-malone

SNEAK PEEK: FOXY LADY

"I swear he was around here a minute ago," Mrs. Johnson said, irritation edging into her voice as she bent over to look behind the sofa. "See, this is exactly what I'm talking about. He's impossible!"

Sydney Young just laughed, watching the middle-aged woman get to her hands and knees on her living room floor so she could look under an old recliner. Mrs. Johnson was irritated when Syd arrived, and after five minutes of wandering through the house, looking for the little fennec fox, she was verging on incensed.

"It's okay," Syd told her. "He can't have gone too far - we'll find him. What did you say his name is again?"

"Sonic," Mrs. Johnson said, distracted as she peeked behind the entertainment center in the corner of the room. "My youngest took one look at his ears and decided on it. If I have to hear him bickering with his siblings one more time about the fact that Sonic is a hedgehog, not a fox..."

The poor woman was clearly at the end of her rope - and Syd was not surprised. This morning, Mrs. Johnson had called the Western Ohio Wildlife Rehabilitation Center where Syd worked and told the dispatcher that her eldest son had come home with a half-wild fennec fox a month ago. What ensued was four long weeks of destroyed furniture, smelly scent-marked pillows, and nocturnal playtime that kept the whole family up at night.

"It's either me or the fox," Mrs. Johnson had told Tara, the dispatcher on the call. "Somebody has to come out here and get him or I'm letting him loose in the back yard."

The fact that the rehab center wasn't in the business of taking in surrendered pets was completely lost on Mrs. Johnson, and Syd decided that she'd better get out to the woman's house before the poor fennec found himself outdoors and on his own. She'd figure out what to do with him later.

"Sonic," Syd called now, looking behind the drapes and under the dining table. "Come on out, boy. I brought some tasty dried crickets for you."

Mrs. Johnson wrinkled her nose. "Yet another reason

I'll be happy when he's gone. You know he got out of the house one time and dragged a dead mouse under the couch, like he was saving it for later?"

"Kind of like a cat," Syd pointed out, but Mrs. Johnson only rolled her eyes.

"And you'll notice I don't have any of those around here either," she said. "From now on, this house is an herbivores-only zone. I can't take it."

Just then, a little tan blur shot out from under the recliner and streaked across the living room. Perhaps his name wasn't quite so wrong after all. Mrs. Johnson let out a yelp as the fox headed into the kitchen and Syd followed quick behind him with the pet carrier she'd brought along.

"Come on, Sonic," she said. "You've outstayed your welcome here, buddy."

An hour later, Syd was back at the wildlife rehabilitation center - known as WOW among the fifteen or so veterinarians, technicians and office staffers who worked there.

Sonic the fox was sniffing around his new accommodations - a climate-controlled kennel stocked with all the bugs, fresh fruit and chow he could eat. He was ignoring all of it at the moment, too busy coming to terms with the drastic reduction in the size of his environment.

"It's temporary," Syd told him, imagining she could see scorn in those big, jet-black eyes.

"Can we puh-*lease* let him out and play with him?" Tara asked. She had her fingers looped through the chain-link kennel door.

Most of the time when a new animal came to WOW, people sprang into action to take care of it if it was injured or sick, but nobody stood around fawning over new arrivals. But it wasn't every day that they got a fennec, with its enormous satellite dish ears and curious, scheming expressions. When Syd brought Sonic in, everyone stopped and circled around.

"Only if you want to adopt him," Syd teased Tara. "We should let him get used to his surroundings for a bit, and then he'll need a complete check-up. I'm not convinced Mrs. Johnson and her kids did their research, so I'm mostly concerned about possible malnutrition, though he seems healthy enough."

As if to prove her point, the little fox let out a bark and launched himself at the gate, scrambling halfway up it and making Tara squeal with delight before he landed gracefully back on his feet. Then he went over to the bowl in the corner and helped himself to all the bugs in the dish.

"Yup, he's acclimated," Danielle, the director of the rehabilitation center, said with a chuckle before she headed back to her office, wordlessly dispersing the rest of the staff in the process.

Tara followed Syd back to the office side of the building and to her desk, which was within shouting distance of the dispatch station where Tara sat.

The majority of the large, converted warehouse

where they worked was dedicated to the animals - kennels, exam rooms, a surgical suite, and an indoor play area for days when it wasn't possible to take the rescue animals outside for exercise.

The office space wasn't much more than a cluster of desks, the director's office, a conference room and a break room. Hardly anyone ever sat at their desks, but Syd had a few calls to make.

"What are you going to do with him?" Tara asked as Syd sat down.

"We've never had a fennec before," Syd said. "They can't live in the wild around here - much too cold - so we have no choice but to rehome him as a pet. Gotta find somebody who actually knows about foxes though. I don't know where the Johnson kid got Sonic, but he clearly didn't know what he was signing up for."

"Probably some unscrupulous breeder," Tara said, letting out a sigh. WOW didn't see quite as much of that as some of the private practice vets that Syd knew, focusing as they did on wildlife, but she knew it was a problem that was only getting bigger.

The dispatch phone rang and Tara walked away to answer it, and Syd swiveled in her desk chair, picking up her own phone.

Her first call was to a fellow rehabber that she'd met a few years ago at the National Wildlife Rehabilitators' annual symposium who happened to be a fox expert. She filled up an entire page on a legal pad with care, habitat and feeding notes, as well as some criteria that the two of them had come up with to make sure Sonic got placed in the right home.

Lots of room outdoors to play and dig. Climate controlled habitat because fennecs are desert foxes. Willingness to spend time creatively hiding food because foxes are foragers. Commitment to care for Sonic for the next 10+ years.

It was a long list that required a lot more than a typical dog or cat, and on top of that challenge, Syd was used to rehabilitating and releasing - not rehoming. For that reason, her next call was to Parker Rose-Wakefield, a friend who'd been successfully running a rabbit rescue for the last year and a half.

"Hell-" Parker started to answer, then let out a little yelp followed by a laugh before finally finishing the word. "Oh?"

"Hey, Parker, it's Syd Young," Sydney said, then laughed. "What the hell's going on over there?"

"Sorry... I was carrying a rabbit when you called and she decided to take advantage of the distraction to try to climb over my shoulder," Parker explained. "It's okay, Jules caught her."

"Oh good, you're both there," Syd said. Parker's wife was a veterinarian who did a little bit of everything - pets, exotics, large animals - and she'd helped Syd with rescues a number of times around Camden, where all three of them lived. "I could use some advice if you've got the escaped bunny situation under control."

"Sure," Parker said. There was a crackle as she put Syd on speakerphone.

"What's up?" Jules asked.

Syd told them about her newest rescue and explained the particular challenges of taking care of a domesticated fox. "I've never tried to rehome a fox before. I was hoping you'd have some advice."

"Don't give him to any of our clients," Parker said with a laugh. "I don't know foxes but I know they don't mix with rabbits."

"Check," Syd said. "What else?"

"I would insist on a home visit," Jules said. "Since this isn't a typical pet, it's not unreasonable to ask to see the habitat, and you could take Sonic with you to get a feel for the potential adopter's compatibility."

"Yeah," Syd said, distracted as she scribbled down more notes.

"And you said he has behavioral issues, right?" Parker asked.

"That's what Mrs. Johnson said," Syd told her. "But I got the impression that she would have said that about any animal that didn't sit quietly in a corner."

"Well, we've had our fair share of bunnies that were hard to adopt," Parker said, and then she and Jules said in unison, "Cotton." They laughed, then Parker went on. "One thing that's helped a lot is bringing the bunnies into the house for some extra socialization before they're ready to be adopted. If you can, you should make time to play with Sonic, figure out what his challenges are and get started on correcting them. He doesn't have to be perfectly trained, but it'll make him much more adoptable if he's friendly and used to people."

Syd nodded along the whole time. "That makes a lot of sense. Maybe I can give Tara a new desk mate."

"What about me?" Tara called when she heard her name.

Syd covered the receiver and called back, "I said *Tara wants to adopt this fox, I can tell*."

"Would that I could," Tara called back. "My mom says if I bring one more animal home, I have to move out."

Syd uncovered the phone and said, "Thanks so much for the advice, guys. I appreciate it."

"Any time," Jules said. "Hey, wanna get dinner with us sometime this weekend?"

"Sure," Syd said. "Just text me."

She hung up and sat back in her chair for a minute. Half of her was strategizing the best way to make sure Sonic's stay at WOW was as short as possible, and the other half was thinking ahead to dinner with Jules and Parker.

She loved them both and they always had a good time, but it was impossible not to feel like a third wheel while eating dinner with a pair of newlyweds. It sometimes felt like being a voyeur in the middle of someone else's date, and even though Parker and Jules never meant to make her feel that way, there was nothing two blissfully happy people could do to contain that love that seemed to ooze into every word and gesture.

It was sweet, it was the teeniest bit sickening, and hanging out with Jules and Parker was one of the rare times that Syd was reminded of how single she was.

Syd spent the next few weeks trying unsuccessfully to find a new family for Sonic. She called every vet in her address book looking for leads. She'd asked all her friends to spread the word. She exhausted the list of possible foster families that her fox expert friend had given her, but no one had room for Sonic.

She'd even put up an ad on Craigslist in a last-ditch attempt to find the perfect person who was waiting out there for Sonic to find her. That turned out to be a massive error in judgment - Syd was inundated with calls from people who knew less than she did about foxes and clearly weren't up to the task.

In the meantime, Syd spent as much time as she could with Sonic in between rescues and her other rehab work.

She fed him his breakfast at the beginning of every shift and made sure he got a nutritious snack of tasty, crunchy bugs every afternoon.

She made toys and games to keep him occupied in the otherwise sterile and dull confines of his kennel, and she made sure he had plenty of playtime in the big outdoor pen at the back of the building.

Whenever he saw her coming, Sonic would climb the gate of his kennel, his bushy tail swishing back and forth in greeting. He was kind of a maniac, turning into a blur of sandy fur the moment Syd let him out, and she had to constantly monitor him to make sure he didn't dig his way under the fence when they were outside, but once he got tuckered out, he'd curl up on her lap and let her scratch behind his ears.

One afternoon when the sun was baking down on them and Sonic was napping with his chin up on her thigh, Syd snapped a picture with her phone and posted it to Facebook with the caption, *Not gonna lie, he's a handful, but fox snuggles are the best. They could be yours if you're ready to adopt ;)*

She wasn't really expecting to get any nibbles from it, but a few minutes later, her phone pinged and Sonic's head shot up, his ears alert.

"It's just a Facebook notification, buddy," Syd told him with a snort. "You'll get used to these things once you're cultured."

She picked up her phone and that proved to be too much activity for Sonic. He shot up and darted across the pen, racing through the grass like his tail was on fire. Syd laughed and checked the notification.

Looks like he already found his ideal snuggle buddy.

It was from Marley, a vet that Syd had known since school. She laughed, brushing it off, but then a minute later, Parker chimed in to agree with her.

Just take him home already - you know you love him.

Syd watched Sonic race around the enclosure. He jumped up on things and kicked off of them, bounded off the fences, and even darted across her lap when he'd completed the circle and went out for another one.

She let out a sigh.

She worked eighty hours some weeks and she was on call more often than not. There was dust an inch thick in some unused spaces in her house - that was how much time she spent there. She didn't even have time for a girlfriend... how the hell was she supposed to make time for a half-wild fox?

But when Sonic had spent all his energy tearing across the pen, he wound up back in her lap. This time, he crawled onto her outstretched legs, his body warming her shins and his chin resting just above her knees.

He looked up at her with kind, loving eyes, and as she reached down to pet his big, fuzzy ears, she sighed again and said, "Damn it. I guess you're coming home with me, you adorable little bastard. You really know how to pour it on thick, don't you?"

He looked innocently up at her and in her mind, Syd started working out a new problem. What would she need to fox-proof her house? How could she build an inescapable outdoor pen for Sonic to be comfortable in during her long hours at work?

And what the hell would her brand-new neighbors, who'd just moved in last week and who Syd hadn't had time to introduce herself to yet, think of a fox enclosure popping up in her back yard?

The answer to that last one was obvious. They'd think she was a crazy fox lady.

Read Foxy Lady on Amazon

LESFIC BOOK CLUB

Calling all lesfic lovers!

Join us for a monthly book club, talk to your favorite lesbian fiction authors, check out our growing community of published and aspiring writers, and hang out in daily chats with fellow lesfic lovers. Check out the group at http://lesficlove.com

Made in the USA
Monee, IL
24 December 2020